CAGE

ED GORMAN

Ed Gorman became a full-time writer after twenty years in advertising, and is acknowledged as being one of the world's leading writers of dark suspense. He is the founder and editor of *Mystery Scene* and lives in Cedar Rapids, Iowa with his wife, novelist Carol Graham. Amongst his other novels are *Night Kills*, *Blood Red Moon*, *Hawk Moon* and *Harlot's Moon*.

Praise For Ed Gorman

"Books like this are what inspired me to become a writer in the first place."

–Dean R Koontz

"Gorman has a way of getting into his characters, and they have a way of getting into you."

– **Robert Bloch**, author of *Psycho*

"Gorman pulls things off with sleek bravura, reclaiming the field from the legions of cardboard cutout serial killers."

– **Time Out**

Ed Gorman

CAGE OF NIGHT

CT Publishing

First published in Great Britain by CT Publishing, 1998.
This edition 1998 CT Publishing.
Copyright © Ed Gorman 1998

A CIP catalogue record for this book is
available from the British Library.

ISBN 1-9020020-2-4

9 8 7 6 5 4 3 2 1

Book design and typography by Crow Media Design.
Printed and bound in Great Britain by Caledonian
International Book Manufacturing, Bishopbriggs, Glasgow.

IN MEMORY OF ROBERT BLOCH

CAGE OF NIGHT

*"Darkness
dwells
within even the best of us.*

*In the worst of us,
darkness not only dwells,
but
reigns."*

Dean Koontz, "Down in the Darkness"

Part One

Richard Mitchell, KNAX-TV:

"The big question here today is will the equipment work effectively? Not many people will forget what happened seven months ago when another man was executed in this prison. Lethal injection is supposed to be the most humane way to put somebody to death, but last time something went wrong with the hypodermic needle. The prisoner's entire nervous system was paralysed, but he didn't die immediately. In fact, it took him forty-eight minutes to die, and the medical examiner listed the cause of death as suffocation. A pretty grim way to go. Everybody's hoping for a much quicker and more humane execution today."

Tape 4-D, June 23. Interview between Attorney Susan Amerson and her client in the Clark County jail (A=Attorney, C=Client.)

A: I want you to tell me about the alien again.

C: You don't believe me, do you?

A: I thought we worked through this already. I'm not your enemy. I'm your friend. I'm trying to help you.

C: But you don't believe me.

A: (Long sigh) I want you to tell me about the alien.

From a Police Report – August 23, 1903

Officer Henley became very ill when we reached the victim up in the attic. He had to go home for the rest of the day. That's why I, the junior officer, am writing this report to you, Chief Sullivan. The thing is, he cut off her head. That's what made Henley so sick, We opened the attic door and looked up the stairs and there was her head, very bloody and with the eyes torn out, sitting right at the top of the stairs. Henley never did go upstairs. He went down to the main floor and vomited. Then it was left to me to go upstairs and find the rest of her body.

1

I guess by now you pretty much know what happened the last year or so in the Valley here. My name is Spence.

All I can hope is that you'll give me time to tell my side of things. Nobody ever did. Not the cops, not the press, not even my own parents. They all just assumed –

Well, they assumed wrong, each and every one of them.

I'm here to tell you about Cindy Marie Brasher.

Night we met, I was twenty-one and just out of the Army, and she was eighteen and had just been voted Homecoming Queen. She was not only good looking, she was popular, too.

Which is something I'd never been. Popular, I mean.

Maybe I wasn't an outright nerd but I came pretty close. The few dates I'd had hadn't exactly been spectacular successes, and the only kids who asked me to hang around were the ones I always saw out at the mall playing video games and buying science fiction paperbacks. I was buying them, too.

I wasn't ready for college – mediocre grades, and no real desire to go – so I enlisted in the Army. I have to admit, I had pretty fancy dreams. I'd come back looking like a movie star and possessing secret knowledge of at least forty-eight ways to kill a man in less than ten seconds.

Well, I wasn't quite a movie star when I came back but I had shed my baby fat and my zits, and I had become a fair sandlot softball player. I still knew only one way to kill a man, and that was with a gun. The Army had turned me into a pretty decent marksman.

Right here I probably should tell you about Josh, my younger brother. I wouldn't have met Cindy Brasher that night if he hadn't taken me to the kegger.

When I left for the Army three years earlier, Josh was a skinny, gangly kid who spent most of his time in front of the

14

TV screen watching *The Three Stooges* and really dorky horror movies. He was even more of a social and academic disaster than I'd been.

But while I was gone, frog became prince. He became one of the three best forwards in state basketball, he developed into a damned good looking kid with all the social skills I lacked, and he managed to accomplish these feats while maintaining a 3.9 grade average.

It was supposed to be the other way around, wise older brother teaching naive younger brother about the ways and wiles of life...

But in my case, I found myself a little intimidated by my brother. We'd be walking down the street and at least half the people we'd meet, young and old alike, would stop to make a fuss over him, to compliment him on his basketball playing, or to tell him how much they liked the particular shirt he was wearing, or to invite him to some function he clearly didn't want to go to.

Josh always dutifully introduced me, making a big thing about my Army years, but very few of his admirers paid me more than passing interest. Josh was the star here.

I suppose he was feeling sorry for me the night he invited me to the kegger out in Hampton Woods. I was just sitting around the kitchen table talking with Mom and Dad about my plans to start community college next spring.

He came in the kitchen and said, "Why don't you go to that kegger with me tonight?"

I laughed. "You want to invite Mom and Dad, too? Don't you think I'm a little old for a high school kegger?"

He grinned. "Everybody'll be so drunk they won't even notice how old you are."

Mom frowned, obviously thinking of drunken teenagers driving cars. Josh leaned over and gave her a kiss and charmed her worries away. "Just kidding, Mom." Then: "C'mon, brother. You're going with me."

15

"Go on, Spence," Dad said. "You might have a good time." He winked at Josh. "Anyway, you'll get to see that Cindy Brasher. She's the Homecoming Queen and a real beauty."

"I'm sort of surprised they let her be queen," Mom said. "You know, after her troubles last year and all."

I wanted to ask what kind of troubles but Josh was tugging me away. He was like somebody from a different species – tall, poised, good looking, self-confident. Sometimes it didn't do my ego a whole lot of good to stand next to him.

"We'll be home early," Josh shouted merrily as we walked through the house to the bedroom we shared. "No later than dawn for sure."

Then he laughed so Mom and Dad would know he was joking.

In my room, while I changed shirts and pants, he filled the wallet I'd bought for his birthday last week. He dumped the contents of the old wallet on the dresser top, then transferred everything to the new wallet.

"You ever use these?" he said, flashing me a kind of condom I'd never seen before. It came in an aqua wrapper. "French ticklers. Girls love 'em."

I wondered if I should tell him, then decided against it. He'd only feel sorry for me – or think something was wrong with me – if I told him I was a twenty-one-year-old virgin.

In the car, a convertible a jock-happy Pontiac dealer let him drive gratis, we rolled through the warm, smoky October night with the top down and the radio loud.

"You dig chicks, right?" he said.

"Sure," I said. "Why?"

"Just wondered. I mean, you never have any dates."

"Guess I just haven't found anybody to date yet. I've only been home two weeks."

"I'm going to find somebody for you."

I almost laughed. He was still my little brother, despite his size and physical acumen, and here he was conducting a father-son conversation with me. And he was the father.

"I can probably find my own."

"You mind if I say something?"

"Be my guest."

"The way you dress, and your hair —"

"Bad, huh?"

"Real bad. No offence, I mean."

I felt a kind of isolation, then. I'd never fit into any kind of social group before and apparently I wasn't going to start fitting into any now. Not even one that included my own brother.

"How about if I send you down to Peyton's?"

"The men's store?"

"Yeah. Peyton's a big basketball booster. He lets me charge a lot of clothes. He says as long as I score 30 points a game I don't have to worry about paying him back. I'll see if he'll let you put some clothes on my account. Then I'll take you over to King's."

"What's King's?"

"This styling salon."

"Oh, like a barber."

He shook his head. "That's why your hair looks like that, brother. Because you go to a barber instead of a styling salon."

I tried to make a joke of it even though he was starting to irritate me some. "I guess I've got a lot to learn."

He said, quite seriously, "Yeah, brother, you do."

2

Back in my high school days, getting invited to keggers out at Hampton Woods meant that you had been accepted by the popular kids.

I suppose because I'd never been invited, I'd created this picture of a kegger that looked like a beer commercial on TV – you know, lots of attractive young people having a good time being attractive and young.

There were probably fifty cars parked in a fallow cornfield surrounding the edge of the woods that ran alongside the river. You could hear the music from a half mile away. The moonlight gave everything a slightly dangerous, nocturnal feeling.

Josh parked his convertible and we started walking to the edge of the river, where most of the people had congregated.

But before we got there, we saw a small circle of teenage boys forcing themselves to throw up.

"Puking contest," Josh explained as we passed them.

So much for my image of attractive young people having a good time being attractive and young.

A bonfire next to the water's edge threw flickering golden images high into the autumn trees. All I could think of was the war fires Indian tribes used to have on these plains in the early part of the last century. The electric guitar had replaced the war drum.

There had to be a hundred people gathered around the fire. Some were drinking, some were toking on joints, some were making out, some were arm wrestling, some were just sitting very stoned and glassy-eyed and staring up at the bright prairie stars that covered the cloudless night.

Oh, yes, and some were puking.

This time there wasn't any contest. This time it was simply a matter of kids being genuinely sick. The girls generally found this repellent – making noises like 'issh' and 'iccck' and 'oh shit!' – while the boys, being boys, seemed to find the vomiting hilarious.

18

Josh mattered.

I saw that the moment we stepped into the light of the bonfire. People talking paused to look at him; maybe half a dozen kids surged forward to speak to him and touch him in some way; and three different people got him dripping paper cups of beer from the three huge kegs that had been neatly arranged on top of a picnic table.

Josh didn't forget about me.

"This is my brother, everybody," he said. "He just got back from the Army, and he's got some great stories to tell. Right, brother?"

"Yeah," I said, finding a stupid grin on my face, making the "Yeah" sound as if I'd maybe stopped some spies from sneaking into secret Army installations. Or led some kind of guerrilla operation that not even the Senate knew about.

But about the only stories I knew had to do with the night our barracks ran out of toilet paper, and the night that Southern kid went crazy and destroyed the communication shack, after learning that his girlfriend back home had a new boyfriend – a black boyfriend.

"Hey, brother here doesn't have a brewski," Josh said.

At which point three or four kids dashed to the kegs to get me one.

Once my hand was filled, Josh said, "I'm going to check out the chicks. Why don't you just sort of mingle around, you know?"

"Sure," I said, wanting to smile.

When Josh was looking for girls, he didn't want me around. Not with my clothes and my haircut.

I found a tree stump on the edge of darkness and sat there. I could watch the moonsilver river and listen to the barn owls in the darkness on the far shore. I'd never been to a kegger out here, but I had spent a lot of time in these woods. I used to be a hunter and a fisherman until I started feeling sorry for the animals I killed. They had a right to live same as I did. Then I just came to the woods and walked around. That's one of the nice things about not being popular. You have plenty of time on your hands.

Cindy Brasher and her boyfriend got there about twenty minutes after we did.

Her boyfriend, who stood six two easily and who had rough good looks, stirred up the same kind of commotion Josh had.

People encircled him, giving him beers, clapping him on the back, breaking out in laughter at just about everything he said.

But it was Cindy who I really watched.

She wasn't a classic beauty, I suppose, her features not quite fitting together, but there was a strange yearning in the eyes – a sadness that contrasted with the constantly smiling sensual mouth – that I found touching and erotic. She wore a blue sweater and jeans, nothing fancy, and had a plucky little blue barrette in her dark hair. She also had an exceptionally fine body, one a bit on the slender side but full in the hips and breasts. She was every girl who'd ever broken my heart without knowing it. Back in high school, I could fall in love with girls merely by passing them in the halls.

She had her own groupies, girls and boys alike, but she seemed curiously disinterested in them. She looked around constantly. That sense of yearning for something was in her eyes again.

"You think you could kill somebody?" the kid asked.

"I'm not sure."

"I could."

"Oh?" I said.

"Yeah. My old man was in 'Nam. He killed five people and he said it was easy and he said he didn't regret it at all."

"Well, well."

"He said it was him or them."

"Yeah, probably," I said.

"I wish I coulda been in 'Nam."

20

"You missed out on all the fun, huh?"

"My old man used to tell me about R&R. You know, when they'd take you out of the jungle and send you to Australia or somewhere for a couple weeks vacation. You wouldn't believe some of the stories, man. My old lady gets real pissed when he tells the one about him sleeping with three different Oriental chicks in the same night."

He was the first one of the kegger to come over to my tree stump and talk to me. He was skinny, and he wore a ponytail, and he had matching tiger tattoos on his forearms.

He put out his hand. He was very earnest about it. "My name's Ken, man."

"Nice to meet you, Ken."

"I'm gonna do what you did."

"Oh?"

"Day we graduate, I'm goin' to the recruiter's office and join up." He shook his head. "I just wish there was a war on. I mean, that'd be the fun part of being in the service. War, and shit like that. You know what I mean?"

"Army's a bunch've pussies," said another kid who stood nearby.

He was big and he was mean and he'd probably had enough beer to get three or four people my size good and drunk for two days. He was trying to impress everybody by walking around without his shirt on. He looked to be at least as dumb as he was drunk.

"Pussies," he repeated.

"Fuck yourself, Sullivan," Ken said. "My old man ain't no pussy, I'll tell you that."

"The hell if he ain't," Sullivan said. "And you're a pussy and so's this asshole."

The asshole in question was yours truly.

In the service I'd learned how to handle myself pretty well. But being called an asshole by an asshole like this didn't seem worth fighting over.

21

Ken was of a different mind. "You call my old man a pussy again, Sullivan, I'll punch your face in."

The beers went pluming into the air as Sullivan's arms sprung out just far enough to grab Ken by the throat and lift him up into the air. Sullivan was a lot more formidable than I'd given him credit for.

Most of the people around the campfire were already shouting for Sullivan to put him down. But that wasn't going to happen. Ken's face was already dark with blood.

"Put him down," I said.

"Little faggot fucker," Sullivan said to Ken, choking him some more. He didn't seem to have heard me.

I hit him as hard as I could in the kidney and I was gratified to hear him groan immediately. I followed up with two more punches to the same area. His grip had slipped but he still had a loose grasp of Ken so I slammed a fist hard into his ear.

This definitely got his attention.

He not only dropped Ken but turned to start for me. But he was too fat and too stupid to protect himself so I planted the steel-toe of my boot right into his crotch and as he dropped to his knees, I kicked him hard on the jaw for good measure.

He started vomiting right away, and crying, but they were tears of rage and frustration. I'd scared him and that was an awful thing for somebody like Sullivan to acknowledge.

I went over and took Ken by the elbow and dragged him down toward the river, picking us up two fresh beers as we passed a big iced aluminium tub.

I said, eager to change the subject, "Who's that girl?"

"I just want to thank you, man."

"Just watch yourself. He's probably going to take another run at you tonight."

"Or you."

"Yeah," I said. "Maybe." Then, "Who's that girl?"

"Which one?"

"Blue sweater."

"Cindy Brasher." He grinned at me slyly. "Like to get a sniff of her panties, wouldn't ya?"

He was one elegant sonofabitch, no doubt about it.

"She's pretty."

"I wouldn't say that in front of David Myles."

"That's the guy she's with?"

"Yeah. Captain of the football team. Has about three colleges a week fly out here to try and recruit him. He's also a real bad drunk. Mean." He hoisted his paper cup of beer. "You want to share a joint?"

"No, thanks."

He looked at Cindy some more. "The funny thing is, you'd never know she was in the nut house most of last year."

"The nut house?"

"Yeah. You know, mental hospital."

"For what?"

He shrugged. "Her parents are kind of upper-class, or think they are. You know, they think their shit don't stink. Anyway, her parents inherited the old Miller mansion and moved here two years ago."

"Why did Cindy go to the mental hospital?"

"Nobody's real sure. Just one day in school she started talking to somebody that nobody else could see. And so the principal took her out of class and called her parents, and next thing everybody knew Cindy was in the nut house. She's got great tits, doesn't she?"

The next couple of hours confirmed my suspicions that I hadn't missed anything by not being invited to keggers.

A plump girl stripped down to her bra and panties and did an 'Indian' dance in front of the fire, while a number of boys without dates found ways to grab cheap feels. A very drunk kid climbed a tree and promptly fell out and started sobbing until I suggested that somebody should maybe take him to the hospital. You could see raw white bone sticking out of his right arm. A hospital was probably a good idea. A kid with an acoustic guitar tried to sing a few songs. He had a decent enough voice but nobody was up for the kind of mordant folk songs he'd written, most of them about buddies of his who'd overdosed on one drug or another, and girls who'd dumped him.

The lucky kids were scattered through the woods making love.

I went down a narrow dark path a few times to take a leak and heard a symphony of ecstasy from behind the bushes and undergrowth.

Being a twenty-one-year-old virgin, I felt like a spy. Josh put in various appearances and the kids crowded around him as usual.

He had that quick movie star grin and wave down real good. Somewhere there was an invisible camera snapping all this stuff. That was the impression he gave you, anyway.

Most of the time he was in the woods. He'd found an especially voluptuous girl to spend time with. She looked delighted to be with him. I felt a real jealousy for my brother – my little brother, yet – the geeky little kid I'd left behind a few summers ago when I'd gone to the Army.

Now he was instructing me in the ways of fashion and hairstyles and proper behaviour around nubile young girls.

For a time, I ended up downriver, along the edge of the water, watching an eagle sail past the full silver moon. I wanted to enjoy this moment with nature but all I could think about was Cindy Brasher.

I just kept thinking about those eyes of hers, those sad, spooked eyes, and the time she'd spent in a mental hospital.

I wondered about her. I wondered about her a lot.

3

Toward eleven o'clock it started getting cold, an autumn cold that smelled of leaves burning in the hills, and the first bites of winter wind.

Josh came over to my tree stump several times, once even bringing a girl along, one he intended to set me up with, apparently.

She was beautiful, and she intimidated me, and the way she looked at me I could see that Josh had had to drag her over here.

"Guess how old she is?" Josh said.

"How old?"

"Nineteen. Right, Sharon?"

"Right."

"She's Marcy Daniel's sister. Just back for a long weekend from college. I thought you two might have a brewski together. Huh?"

He kind of gave her a little shove toward me and said, "Have some fun, kids. I'm sure going to."

Then he stopped. "Hey, brother, I hear you beat the crap out of Sullivan tonight."

"I sure gave it a try."

He gave me the thumbs up. "I was thinking about doing it myself. He's a real asshole."

"Yeah, I kinda noticed that."

Then he was gone.

The kids around the big bonfire were getting orgiastic now.

The puking contests had moved up to the river's edge and there'd already been a couple of minor fist fights and the making out had turned pretty heavy, one boy and girl snuggled under a blanket pretty obviously making love.

Sharon, who was a sleek blonde goddess, said, "So you were in the Army?"

"Right."

25

"How come you didn't go to college?"

"Wasn't ready. Now I am. You like college?"

"Not really. Not so far. I want to be a doctor. I'll like it a lot better when I can start my pre-med courses."

A blonde goddess who was going to be a doctor. I decided not to tell her about my plans for community college.

"They look so immature, don't they?" she said.

"Yeah."

"You see that puking contest?"

"Yeah."

"I'm going out with this neurologist. He thinks that boys don't mature until they're in their mid-twenties." She looked at the people around the campfire. "They're also into some pretty terrible stuff."

"Drugs?"

"Drugs, and violence."

"The fights I saw tonight weren't much."

"Not fights. I went into the woods and I saw this boy hit this girl right in the face. I said something to them but they ran away. The Homecoming Queen. I think my sister said her name was Cindy."

"He hit her in the face?"

"Yes, and hard, too."

She drained her paper cup. "Well, I'd better see if I can talk my sister into going home. I don't know why I agreed to come out here in the first place. There wasn't anybody worth meeting."

She blessed me with a smile, and was gone.

I spent the rest of the night looking for Cindy Brasher. I couldn't forget what Sharon had told me about Myles hitting her in the face. Then the two of them running away.

By eleven o'clock, the wind was getting so cold that everybody starting packing up and heading back. Even the guys in the never-ending puking contest had started to look cold.

Josh wasn't back. I was tired and the wind was getting to me.

26

I decided to water some more foliage in the woods. Maybe when I returned, Josh would be there and ready to go.

A lot of the leaves were gone this time of year so the moonlight was bright and strong. I found a big boulder and walked behind it and peed. I was feeling the beer just enough to get that melancholy feeling alcohol always gives me. There was something lonely about the way steam rose off my piss as I peed against the rock. I heard a nearby animal in the undergrowth and sort of envied him. It would be nice not to have deal with the human world sometimes.

I was on my way back to the dying bonfire when I heard the crying. I recognised it right away for what it was and I guess I probably knew who it was, too.

Off-trail was an old line-shack that the electric company people had probably used sixty, seventy years ago when they were stringing wire out here in the boonies.

Now it was all tumbledown, all busted windows and jagged boards,

She sat in the doorway of it, her face in her hands. She wasn't crying hard, it was just a kind of soft, exhausted grief.

She heard the dead leaves crunch beneath my feet and looked up.

"Oh," she said, "hi."

"Hi."

She sniffled and wiped the tears from her eyes with cute little red mittens. I found everything about her cute and fetching and overwhelming. I'd never felt this before and it scared me. It was like driving a car at two hundred miles an hour and all of a sudden the steering goes out and then the brakes go out, too.

"You're Josh's brother."

"Yeah."

"I'm Cindy Brasher."

"The Homecoming Queen."

She laughed. "Big deal, huh?"

"It is a big deal."

She kept her right hand mitten under her eye. When she took it away, I saw why. She had a shiner, and a good one, and it was turning big and ugly already.

"Hey," I said, "what happened?"

"Oh, I tripped and fell down."

"You did, huh?"

"Yeah."

"You should get some ice on that."

"Ice helps?"

"Helps a lot. If you get it on soon enough."

"Maybe I will."

In two more steps I was next to her and then before I knew what I was doing, I knelt down beside her and touched my finger to her eye.

"Wow," I said. "You really hurt yourself. You got a headache?"

"I had a little one, I guess."

I couldn't believe that I was touching her this way.

"You're really gentle. Your hand, I mean."

"Thanks."

"I really like gentle things," she said. There was a dreamy, far-off quality to her voice now, as if she were addressing not me but somebody else.

"Hey asshole, what the hell're you doing?"

Before I could even turn around to see him, David Myles had grabbed the back of my coat and lifted me up off the ground and started shaking me.

"Just because you're Josh's asshole brother doesn't cut any shit with me, you understand?"

By now, even though I was shaking, I'd gathered myself enough to kick him sharply in the shin. He cried out and released me when my heel met his shinbone. I turned to face him. He was protecting himself, but I got him a nice solid one right on the nose.

Then she was between us, screaming for us to stop, shouting

to Myles that it was all her fault, and frantically pushing me away.

"Just get out of here," she said. "I shouldn't have been talking to you. This is all my fault."

"I ever see you touching her again, jerk-off, you're going to be very, very sorry. You understand?"

He wanted another go at me and I guess I wanted another go at him, too. Our dislike of each other was immediate and profound. But she was still screaming to keep us apart.

And then they were gone. I stood in the silver moonlight thinking of how tender and warm her cheek had felt to my touch. I was back in that car again, two hundred mph and no brakes. Out of control.

"You have a good time?" Josh said.

"Yeah."

He looked over at me.

"Yeah, you sound like it. Two fights in one night, huh? My brother the badass. Who would've thought?"

"You've got some nice friends."

"A lot of them are just silly-ass little kids." He grinned at me. We had the top down and were freezing our balls off. It was some kind of macho rite. We were going maybe eighty mph. "You got the hots for Cindy Brasher, huh?"

"You're full of shit."

"Hey, man, it's all right. Lots of guys have the hots for Cindy. Just watch out for Myles. He's going to come back for round two."

"Yeah," I said. "I kind've figured he might."

"Well, brother, I got some bad news for you," Josh said.

"Yeah?"

"Yeah. Most guys at that school, I can kick their butts without breaking a sweat. David Myles, I couldn't kick his butt if I had a gun and he had his hands tied behind his back. He's a real animal. He's a lot tougher when he isn't as drunk as he was tonight."

"How come she goes out with him, anyway?"

He shrugged. Questions about psychology didn't seem to interest him much. "Who knows? Maybe she's nuts. She had some kind of breakdown last year. Ended up in the bughouse. Had those treatments – riding the lightning they call it."

"Electro-shock?"

"Yeah."

"Wow. That's bad shit."

"Tell me about it," Josh said. "Young girl like that, pumping all that voltage into her."

I could barely stand to think about it. Couple guys in the Army had ridden the lightning. It was pretty bad. I just kept thinking of Cindy Brasher, her body dancing around as they shot her up with electricity.

Twenty minutes later, we pulled up in front of our house.

Josh didn't cut the lights.

"You going somewhere?" I said.

"Brother of mine, I've got some sweet young pussy waiting for me. And I'm in a hurry to get to it."

It was funny to me again, me being older and more experienced in many ways. But somehow Josh was senior and I was junior.

"Well, I may still be up when you get home."

He grinned. "Don't count on it."

Richard Mitchell, KNAX-TV:

"One thing the folks at home should understand about this execution today, Paul, is that they've rehearsed it three times a day for the past three days. And I mean, rehearsed it with a stopwatch. The warden says that if everything goes right, the whole thing should take fifty-five minutes. This is counting from the time the prisoner is brought over to the death house to the time the medical examiner pronounces the prisoner dead. The warden wants to make very sure that this operation goes smoothly."

Tape 11-D, August 6; Interview between Risa Wiggins and her client in the Clark County jail.

A: So you definitely heard this – thing?

C: Yes, definitely.

A: It spoke to you.

C: You're just like that other bitch, you don't believe me, do you?

A: I don't like being called names. That's one reason Susan quit the case.

C: I heard the fucking alien, all right? It really exists and it really fucking spoke to me, OK?

4

A freak snowstorm hit two weeks later.

I watched it falling past the front windows of Schroeder's department store. Schroeder's used to be the place that most people bought everything, from their TV sets to their school clothes. It was a four-storey building packed with just about everything you could think of. They'd given extended credit to the farmers who could only pay when the crops came in, and they'd given the men and women who worked out at the vulcanising factory a special ten percent discount because of a bargain they'd struck with the union.

That's how things used to be.

Out here now, the chains have pretty much changed everything.

McDonald's and Burger King have pretty much wiped out the mom and pop diners; the new owners of the three factories drove the unions out when they took over; and Wal-Mart chased away all the department stores.

If you wanted to shop now, you likely went out to the mall. A lot of storefronts downtown were either boarded up or draped in pigeon droppings.

I had two and a half months to go before I started community college so I had to do something. I saw an ad for Schroeder's in the paper and decided to take the job. Josh prepped me. He made me get that haircut he wanted, the one with the sideburns cut straight across near the top of the ear with enough left in back for a fussy little ponytail, and he bought me those clothes he'd promised. I had to admit, I looked better. I'd never have Josh's good looks but at least I had a little style.

Schroeder's turned out to be a depressing place to work. Most of the clerks didn't like me because they were being forced into early retirement with about half the benefits they'd been promised. Old man Schroeder was able to hire me for minimum wage and no benefits whatsoever. I guess they saw me as a kind of scab.

The other thing that was depressing was the store itself. Schroeder hadn't repainted in years. In memory, Schroeder's was this really neat place where Mom and Dad would take me to pick out birthday and Christmas gifts. Every bicycle, every atomic ray gun, every rock and roll album you ever wanted could be found at Schroeder's. It was a magical place.

But not anymore.

Now it was just this old dusty building where the paint was scaling off the walls, and where some of the mannequins had the wrong arms and legs screwed on them, and where the toilets didn't flush so good, and where everybody who worked there seemed old and slow and sad and resentful.

Time crawled in Schroeder's and I was always hoping I could find another job, but I never did.

I was working in the shoe department the first day Cindy Brasher came into the store.

My customer at the moment was a middle-aged guy who was trying to decide if he wanted cordovan or black wing-tips.

Despite what you may hear, men are generally harder to sell than women. Women buy shoes all the time so one more pair isn't a big deal. But men buy shoes only once every few years or so, so they take their time. This guy had been there nearly an hour now. He'd try on the black ones then the cordovan ones then the black ones again, then he'd tell me the colours of his three suits and ask me to help him decide which shoes would be most useful to him.

After I saw Cindy, I didn't give a damn about the guy or his fashion decision.

These days Josh was always kidding me at the dinner table about Cindy. He'd told Mom and Dad that he thought I was in love because every chance I got I managed to ask him a question about her. A lot of the times, I got embarrassed, and Mom would pat my hand and tell Josh to quit picking on me like that. Dad just kept saying, "But she's only eighteen, and you're practically a man."

I hadn't seen her since that night at the kegger.

This afternoon, she wore a fawn-coloured winter coat, and her dark hair was tied back with a red ribbon, and she just broke my fucking heart. There's no other way to say it. When I saw her there I felt love, fear, lust, sorrow, joy. I wanted to laugh and come and cry all at the same time. Her fading shiner made me feel protective of her.

"Maybe the cordovans would be better," the man was saying.

I wanted to get rid of him. Fast.

"I'll tell you what," I said. "Why don't I charge these both to you then you take them home and try them on with your different suits. You keep one pair and bring the other one back."

"Hey, that's a great idea."

I got him up to the cash register, and had his shoes sacked and his charge slip all made up in under a minute. Then I handed him the shoes and walked over to the edge of the department where Cindy was looking at a pair of Capezio flats.

I got right up behind her but then I didn't know what to say. I just sort of froze there.

She smelled beautiful. Some kind of perfume or something. It made me dizzy and horny and melancholy. I was overwhelmed. I had to will my hands not to grab her.

"Aren't you going to say anything?" she said.

She didn't turn around. She just knew I was there.

"Uh, hi."

Then she turned around and she was smiling and she broke my heart for the second time that day.

"I guess I need some new flats."

"Great. We've sure got flats. A lot of them." I was grinning. I was babbling.

"Would you like me to go over and sit down?"

She could see where she had me and she was nice enough to be sweet about it.

"Yeah," I said. "That's a great idea."

I can't tell you about the next few minutes because I can't remember much about them. Somehow I was able to control myself enough to measure her foot, note the three different styles she wanted to try on, and find my way back to the stockroom. I remember watching my hand take down a Capezio box. It was trembling visibly, like a junkie's hand in a bad movie. Then I realised that my whole body was trembling. And that I was covered in this icy sweat. I wondered if I smelled. God, what if I smelled, or my breath was killer-bad, the way it sometimes got?

I did a Shemp on the way out, tripping over a shoebox I'd carelessly left in the aisle.

I stumbled forward, the three boxes flying out of my hands and skidding down the floor.

I imagined that she heard it, was sitting out there when this explosion came from the stockroom, and she thought, "What a dweeb this guy is."

But if she did, she didn't let on.

I came out and sat on my little stool and took the first flat from the first box.

She offered her slender ankle and small foot almost daintily, and when I touched her ankle, I almost broke into tears. I know that sounds phoney and fake but it was true. When I touched her ankle, thin and vulnerable as the ankle of a scrawny colt, I felt I'd never touched anything more precious or sacred in my life.

I slipped the shoe on and she got up and walked around in it and looked at it in the foot mirror and then came back and said, "Would you mind if I tried on the other pair?"

"No problem."

I slipped on a shoe from the next pair.

I was bent over, just taking my horn from the back of her shoe, when she said, "I forgot how gentle your hands are."

I didn't know what to say.

She got up and walked around in the shoe.

I couldn't stop watching her. She'd taken her coat off. She wore a fawn coloured sweater, almost the colour of her coat, and a chocolate brown skirt. Her legs were unimaginably beautiful. Her wrists were just as delicate as her ankles. Her smile was girl and woman at the same time.

"I think I'll take these but I guess I should probably try on that other pair. You're not in a hurry, are you?"

"No hurry at all."

She'd just sat down again, and I was just taking the top off the third box, when I saw her look up and let out a short sigh.

She didn't say anything but I knew something had disturbed her.

"Hey, now there's a real macho job," David Myles said. "Selling ladies' shoes."

She looked flustered and embarrassed as Myles plopped himself down in the chair next to hers.

Myles smirked. "You probably take home some high heels and wear them around the house yourself, don't you, lover boy?"

"If you say one more word, David, I'm really going to get angry. Do you understand me?"

I expected him to say something. No big swaggering football hero was going to let a slender girl talk him down.

But suddenly he looked whipped, silent, and even a little bit afraid of her.

I wondered about the dynamics of their relationship. He wasn't adverse to punching her. Yet she could silence him with just a few sharp words.

"Now I'd like to try on the third one," she said.

I nodded.

I slipped the shoe on.

37

Before, I'd let my fingers linger on her artful ankle. But not now. Myles was watching me. I hated him, but hated myself more for being a dweeb and a coward. It was sort of like with Josh. With three years in the Army behind me, I should have been the tough, confident one. But I wasn't.

She got up and walked around and we both watched her.

He caught me watching her and I looked away from her.

She was his, not mine.

At least, that was his feeling.

She came back and sat down and said, "I think I still like the second ones I tried on better."

"Great."

"Will you take a check?"

I wanted to make a joke about not knowing if I could trust her but when I saw Myles glaring at me, I knew better.

I got her written up and sacked up and handed the shoes over to her.

"If they're a little tight, may I bring them back and have you put them on the stretching machine?"

"Be glad to."

"I really appreciate you being so patient and all."

"My pleasure."

This time, I glared right back at Myles when I spoke.

"Well, take care of yourself," she said, then picked up the shoes and walked out of the department.

They disappeared around the corner. I saw them again when they were outside, walking past the front window.

They were arguing.

She looked very angry.

He looked whipped.

My fingers still burned from touching her ankle. I had never held anything so dear in my life.

5

The next day, I was sitting in a chair in the shoe department waiting for customers to show up.

I sensed somebody behind me suddenly and then a male voice said, "Mirrors are the world, Kull. Gaze into my mirrors, and be wise."

I laughed. I couldn't help it. Only one guy I knew would be crazy enough to quote from a Robert E Howard story this way. I mentioned that in my high school days the only people who asked me to hang out with them were the kids out at the mall who spent most of their time playing video games and reading comic books. The only kid I liked especially was Mike Garrett. Like me, he was a dweeb who didn't want to be a dweeb. All the others pretended to be arrogantly proud of being a dweeb, as if it had been a choice they'd made. One other thing Garrett and I shared was a stone fanaticism for Robert E Howard stories. We practically memorised the damned things. The passage about the mirrors was from *The Mirrors of Tuzun Thune*. Garrett always argued that Kull was a greater Howard creation than even Conan.

I knew I was going to see Garrett when I stood up and turned around.

What I didn't know was that I was going to see Garrett in a policeman's dark uniform.

I guess my first reaction was that it was a gag, that he was all got up to go to a costume party or something.

But then I took more careful note of his Sam Browne belt and the Magnum riding his hip. If this was a joke, it was a damned elaborate one.

I guess the big thing was he was so young. He looked like a kid in his dad's uniform.

"I heard you were back from the Army," Garrett said. "I just got back to town myself yesterday. I called your mom and she said you'd be here."

"Wow, you're really a cop?"

He grinned. He had a kid face except for solemn grey eyes. He was a lousy poker player because you could read him so easily. Right now, his face showed pride.

"Just got out of the police academy in the state capitol," he said. "Graduation was two days ago."

"Wow."

"Even managed to get myself a black belt in karate."

"God, Garrett," I said, "Kull would be proud of you."

He laughed. "Yeah, and so would Conan."

All this was a surprise because Garrett had always been the most cowardly kid I'd ever known. He'd walk blocks out of his way to avoid the local bullies. The only time I'd ever seen him fight, he'd taken one punch, started crying, and fell to the ground.

He wasn't the old Garrett.

He'd beefed up maybe twenty pounds and the grey eyes hinted at a ferocity now. Even the hands looked bigger somehow, more purposeful.

"You working now?" I said.

Shook his head. "Start tonight."

"Bet you're excited." I smiled. "I got it. Why don't you go hassle some of the creeps that used to give us so much grief?"

He didn't return the smile.

In fact, he shook his head.

"That's the one thing I learned at the academy. You can't let your feelings get in the way. Had an old cop tell me that and it made a lot of sense. He said if you let anger get in the way, then you start to bully people. And if you let greed get in the way, then you start getting corrupt. And if you let pride get in your way, then you're never able to admit that you made a mistake on a case. He said the best cops are the ones who are strictly professional. Let their heads tell them what to do, not their emotions. And that's just the way I'm going to be." Then he gave me the kid grin again. "Of course, if one of those old bullies should ever get out of line with me —"

"— hit them a few times for me."

"Exactly."

He looked around the store. "This used to be some place, didn't it?"

"Sure did."

"I remember my mom always bringing me here at Christmas time. One year I pissed on Santa's lap."

"Nice kid."

"So how'd you like the Army?"

"It was all right."

"Your mom says you're going to the community college?"

"Yeah, next spring."

"Great."

I think it was about then that we both started realising that the old friendship wasn't quite there any more. We were different people now. Quoting Kull and talking about the old days could only take you so far.

We fell into an uncomfortable silence and then he said, "Well, I'd better head over to the station. Got a lot of things to do before tonight."

"It was really great seeing you, Mike."

"Yeah, it was. We should go get a pizza sometime."

"Right. Talk about Conan."

"And Kull." He frowned. "My mom got rid of all my paperbacks."

"Mine did, too," I said. "When I was away in the Army."

"I'll bet some of those old ones with Frazetta covers are worth a lot of money today."

"Man, they were beautiful, weren't they?" I said.

"Yeah," he said, "yeah, they really were." And for a moment there, he sounded as sentimental as I felt at the moment. It's funny how you can get melancholy about the person you used to be, as if that person were a separate person from you.

"Let's have that pizza," I said.

"I'll give you a call," he said.

And then I wanted to smile but I knew better.

I couldn't help it.

He still looked like a kid in that uniform, the pug nose and freckled face.

Even with the Sam Browne and the Magnum, he looked like a kid.

6

About twenty minutes before closing time, everybody in the store would start to get bundled up for the trip outside into early winter. Halloween had barely passed and now jolly snowmen with cocked top hats and knowing smiles kept sentry duty all over town. Yellow road graders with big yellow insect eyes roared through the night. And young people who were in love had snowball fights up and down the night time streets.

After I counted the money and took it upstairs to the accounting department, I finished closing up the shoe department for the night.

I was just pushing the fitting tools underneath their chairs, so the cleaning lady wouldn't have to bother with them when she was vacuuming, when the stout and unfriendly woman who worked in women's apparel came over to me.

She was sixty going on thirty. When I was little she'd been the local femme fatale. She and her husband used to drive around in big ass cars like local celebrities. They still had that air about them, being special and important. She had hair that had been peroxided so much it had the dead, dry texture of a wig. She usually wore cream coloured suits meant to hide her bulges. And she effected a kind of Marilyn Monroe gush when she spoke, all dramatic whispers. I managed to hate her and feel sorry for her at the same time. Her feelings for me were much simpler. She just hated me.

"You had a visitor. I forgot to tell you."

"A visitor?"

"A girl."

"A girl. Did she have a name?"

"That cute one who was Homecoming Queen."

"Why didn't you tell me?"

"I don't like that tone of voice."

I sighed. There was no point in arguing with her.

"When was she here?"

43

"Over your dinner hour."

"What did she say?"

"That she was looking for you and would I give you that message." A coy smile: "I'm kind of surprised she'd stop by, knowing the kind of guys *she* could get."

She'd always be in high school, this one, where the popular kids never had truck with the unpopular ones. I walked away.

It was cold in the parking lot.

I spent two minutes scraping rough ice from my windshield. In the meantime, I let the motor run so the car would get warm. Dad had loaned me enough money to buy an old junker Chevrolet. It'd get me back and forth to college. If the heater never exactly warmed up, I had an old blanket on the back seat I could throw over my legs when the thermometer hit zero.

The seat was cold on my butt and legs, and the motor kept dying, but I got out of the parking lot and onto the street. Though the plough had been down here, the wind was blowing snow hard enough that I had to use windshield wipers. The mercury vapour lights gave the downtown a flat, sterile look. With all the empty storefronts, it resembled one of those places in the rust belt where towns just collapsed after the steel mills shut down.

I fishtailed to a stop at every light. There wasn't much traffic. I passed a cop car parked at a corner. I could see a cop-shape inside but I couldn't make out the face. I wondered if it was Garrett. His first night.

I didn't want to go home. I had absolutely no place else to go but ever since I'd heard that Cindy had stopped by, a terrible restlessness had come over me. I wanted to tell somebody about her. I'd never had a girl come and ask for me before, and certainly never one as beautiful as Cindy.

But where would I go?

I passed a Pizza Hut. The parking lot was crowded with the

kind of cars kids drive. I pulled in. In high school, I never went to the places where the popular kids hung out. It always embarrassed me to sit in a booth and watch the golden ones having their fun, as if I'd do anything just to be near them in some way. I was pathetic enough then.

But Cindy had stopped by for me. That gave me a kind of prestige, even if nobody else knew about it.

I had a *right* to go in the god damned Pizza Hut and sit there with the popular kids. I had a right.

The experience was pretty much the same as it had been back in my high school days. I took a two-seat table in the back and sat there and ate a small cheese pizza by myself. From what I could see, I was the only person in the whole place alone. People looked at me sceptically, as if I had a disease or was going to mug them in the parking lot. The really popular kids merely looked through me. I lived in another dimension. I wasn't there.

He came in just as I was finishing the pizza. He threw the door back and stood just inside, glaring around. He had a lot of snow on his hair and the shoulders of his letter jacket. He was pretty pissed, no doubt about it.

He started walking up and down the aisles, searching. When he got to me, he just sort of snorted and shook his head. I wasn't even worth real contempt. He smelled of cold air and hot sweat and expensive after-shave.

By now, a lot of people were watching him.

Not every night a football star like David Myles comes into the Pizza Hut storming up and down the aisles, looking as if he's ready to kill someone.

When he got to the back of the place, he walked straight up to the women's toilet, tore open the door and stalked inside.

A few seconds later, a frightened but silent older woman came out, tugging her skirt down.

The manager looked at the assistant manager and then the manager gave the assistant manager a little shove.

You go tell him to get the hell out of there, I could hear the manager saying. Bravely.

But Myles was out by the time the assistant manager reached the women's door.

Myles glared at all the diners again, and then headed for the exit door.

Then he was gone and everybody put their heads together speculating on who he'd been looking for. They hadn't done any speculating while he was here. They knew better.

I finished up, left a tip, got out of there.

By the time I reached my junker, snow and ice had buried the roof and windows again. I was in a far dark corner of the lot and the drifts seemed to be worse here. I could barely see for all the blowing snow.

I got the scraper from the front seat and went to work.

A few minutes later, I backed out of the parking lot and drove back on to the street.

I was just pulling up to a stop light when a voice from the back seat said, "Find someplace dark where we can park. I need to talk to you."

I was scared until I realised that I recognised the voice. I looked in the back seat and then on the floor. She'd pulled the cover down over her. Now her head stuck up through the folds of the blanket, a chick being hatched.

"He'll kill me if he finds me," she said. "You have to help me."

7

It wasn't exactly a great night to drive around, not in an old junker anyway.

I kept to dark side streets. I thought of going out into the country but it would be too easy to end up in a ditch.

We skidded a lot and ran up into kerbs and even made a few unexpected U-turns. And we froze. The heater still wasn't working properly. I kept having to scrape off the inside of the windshield.

She stayed in the back seat, tucked in the corner, scrunched down so that nobody could see her from the outside.

"I'm sorry I dragged you into this. Now he'll be mad at you."

I was afraid of Myles, no doubt about it. But it was the flattery thing again. I just felt so damned proud to be associated with her in any way – a girl like her asking a guy like me for help – that I was happy to be in the middle of it.

"He really does want to kill me."

"Not actually kill you," I said.

"Kill me."

I glanced in the rear-view mirror. "You really think so?"

"You don't know what he's like. Nobody does except me. He's – done lots of things that people don't know about."

"Like what?"

"I'd better not say."

"But serious things."

"Very serious things. The *most* serious things."

Most of the houses were dark. People huddled beneath their winter blankets in their winter beds. The snow kept falling. The only ones who'd be happy would be the kids. There likely wouldn't be school tomorrow, not if the snow kept up this way. There was no greater gift to a little kid than a snow day. A whole free day to sled and build snowmen and have snowball fights.

"Should I take you home?"

"No. That's one of the places he'll be watching."

"Then where should we go?"

"I have a friend – Tiffany Welles. She lives a couple of blocks from here. They've got an open garage in the back that they never use. We can pull in there for a while."

The garage smelled of car oil and old rotting wood. I had to shut off the motor. With the fumes and all, it was too dangerous to leave running.

She climbed up into the front seat with me.

"You mind if I smoke?"

"Fine."

"You can share mine."

"No, thanks. I'd just embarrass myself."

"How come?"

"In the Army I tried to smoke. You know, big tough guy. All I ever did was cough and get kind of queasy."

"You have to get past that."

I suppose it was kind of funny. I was willing to risk Myles' wrath by hiding her but I wasn't willing to share her cigarettes.

She smoked two cigarettes in a row. She was very nervous. We didn't talk much. Through a dusty garage window I watched the snow fall outside.

I could smell her perfume. It made me yearn for her, ache for her.

"You think you'd ever go out with me?" she said. I looked at her.

"Are you kidding?"

"Huh-uh."

"Sure I'd go out with you."

"I'm going to break off with David. I really am."

She lay her head back against the seat and took another drag of her cigarette.

"I just don't know why you'd want to go out with somebody like me."

It was a pretty cheap ploy, getting her to tell me what a great and desirable guy I was.

– Who wouldn't go out with you? she'd say. A strong, handsome, sexy hunk like you? You're the quiet kind, Spence, the kind girls don't notice right away. But when they *do* notice you...

But she didn't say that.

"It was your hand."

"My hand?"

"When you touched my eye that night."

"Oh."

"Nobody's ever touched me like that before."

I guess I didn't know what she was talking about.

"It was like for the first time in my life somebody was really touching *me*. Like they really understood me. Like *you* really understood me, Spence."

I just sat there with my hard-on and my heart scared of being broken and all these crazy dreams about the two of us together.

"You really think we'll go out?" I said.

She laughed softly. "Yes, I really do."

"God."

"I can't wait until David finally leaves me alone."

Then she kissed me.

It happened just that fast, and just that unexpected. She'd managed to put her cigarette out without my knowing it, and then she leaned over and took my face between her two hands, and then she kissed me, her face smelling of cologne and cold and utterly perfect high school flesh, and then she took my right hand and slid it inside her coat and covered one of her breasts with it, and I really thought I was going to lose it right then and there, I was so god damned happy and god damned excited I absolutely didn't know what to do with myself.

And then it was over, far far sooner than it should have been, and she said, "I better go home."

"Won't he be there?"

"Eventually, yeah. But I may as well get it over with."

"You said he'll try and kill you."

"If I can make it inside to my dad, I'll be fine. My dad doesn't want me to see him anymore, anyway."

She leaned back again. "God, I'm just so glad your car was at Pizza Hut when I was running away from him. I saw you riding around the other day and recognised it."

"You jumped out of his car?"

"Yes. And just started running. Then I saw your car."

I started the motor.

"I'm glad you saw my car, too," I said.

I stayed to the back streets, taking her home. She lived in the wealthy area of town. Her father ran the stock brokerage downtown. Even against the snowy night, her Tudor-style house looked imposing and snug.

I took the driveway right up to the front walk.

"I really appreciate this, Spence."

"My pleasure."

She reached over and set her hand on mine. I thought of a colt again, all small-boned and vulnerable.

"I can't wait to see you again," she said.

"My pleasure."

"Night."

"Night."

She leaned over and gave me a quick kiss on the cheek and then got out of the car.

I watched her let herself into the front door and disappear inside. A light went on, outlined by the mullioned window.

I backed out and got righted on the street and started driving home and that's when I saw the headlights behind me suddenly.

I recognised the dark blue Bronco right away. My old friend David Myles.

He didn't wait long.

He swept right up behind me and started banging into me hard enough to send me skidding down the street.

With all his power and traction, he didn't have any problem starting and stopping when he wanted to.

He controlled me perfectly, letting me stop skidding just long enough to regain control, and then crashing into me again.

A couple of times, I tried surprise turns, anything to get away from him, but they didn't work. He was quick enough to see what I was up to so he'd hit me on the edge of my rear bumper just as I was going into the turn. Then he'd send me skidding again, fishtailing, even turning around completely a few times.

The funny thing was, although I was angry and scared, I also saw this as an admission on his part that he'd lost Cindy Brasher. Otherwise he wouldn't be doing this. And that gave me the flattered feeling again. I'd become one of those chosen. Cindy's kiss, and bringing my hand to her breast, had anointed me.

We went several more blocks this way, short dark side street blocks, with nobody to see us.

But then we reached Bush Avenue, which was the second busiest street in town. It was well-lighted and well-ploughed.

Just as we reached the intersection, he slammed into me again, sending me spinning around completely.

I just had time to glimpse the same police car I had seen earlier tonight. The number was the same: three. I still couldn't see who was inside.

Then I was backtracking the route we'd just taken, back on the dark side streets, headed toward Cindy's house.

Apparently, Cindy's was where he wanted to go because he kept ramming me in that direction. Even when I'd spin out of control, he'd spin back around so that I was pointed in the direction of her house.

The siren started about a block before we reached Cindy's

street. By now, my car wasn't running at all. It was propelled only by his car hurtling into mine.

One siren became two then three.

Myles gave it one last shot. He knocked my car up off the road and on to Cindy's front lawn and right into a snow-laden oak tree.

Lights were on in all the houses.

I saw Cindy and her parents step out on their front porch, Cindy in her street clothes, her parents in pyjamas and robes.

I was just climbing out of my car when the door was ripped open and Myles reached in and grabbed me.

He yanked me out of the car, threw me up against the tree, and started hitting me with a tyre iron. He got me two times on the side of the head before I was able to hit him in the stomach and get him to back off a little. I ducked the next three swings of the tyre iron, landing a good solid punch to his jaw, and then another solid one to his left ear.

I was just getting ready to bring my steel-toed boot up to his crotch when he connected with the tyre iron. This blow drove me to my knees. He swung again immediately but I was able to move under the tyre iron by no more than an inch.

"That's enough, Myles. Hold it right there."

In my delirium and pain, I recognised the voice.

My old Conan buddy, Garrett.

Officer Garrett.

I was making noises that embarrassed me, mewling sounds I guess. I heard Cindy's voice saying, "Is Spence all right? Is Spence all right?"

And I wanted to stop making the noises − the sounds that revealed me to be a coward − but I couldn't somehow.

Then I was crying, just plain little-kid crying, and that was the worst thing of all.

8

The doctor said, "This won't hurt much."

But he lied. It hurt a lot.

Or, correction, *they* hurt a lot: nine stitches on the side of my head.

I sat in a small white room that smelled of medicine and pain. A nurse stayed with me for a while and then there was a knock on the door and Garrett stood in the doorway.

He just looked at me and shook his head. He waited for the nurse to leave and then he came in and closed the door and said, "You look like shit." He was very aware of his uniform as he moved. He hadn't gotten used to the power it gave him yet. He was still at the self-conscious stage.

"Thank you."

"Your car looks like shit, too."

"It looked like shit, anyway."

"We're charging him with assault and battery."

"The way I feel, you should charge him with murder."

"You're not dead."

"The way I feel, I am."

He got a close glimpse of my face and skull. "He sure worked you over."

"He sure did."

"He won't talk to us. His old man's got a lawyer at the jail."

I happened to be staring right at his face when he said it. "It was about the girl, wasn't it? Cindy Brasher."

His whole face changed and something happened to his voice, too. It got a half octave higher, like a kid's.

He'd met Cindy and been properly smitten.

"You talk to her?" I said.

"Yeah. For about half an hour."

"She tell you what happened?"

"Not exactly."

"She was running from him."

53

"Oh?"

He seemed surprised. I wondered why Cindy hadn't told him.

"She just said you took her for a ride and he got mad and followed you."

I decided not to tell him anything more than Cindy had. "Yeah, that was pretty much what happened."

"Nothing else?"

"Nothing else. Why?"

"I don't know. I just got the feeling she wasn't telling me everything. I had a lot of questions I wanted to ask her."

"Yeah?"

"Yeah. Mostly about Myles."

"He in some kind of trouble?"

"Could be."

I laughed, but when I did the stitches pulled and shot pain arcing across the top of my skull.

"You've had a big night," I said.

"Yeah. My first."

"Busting a football hero."

"Lot of people're going to be pissed about that. They play their last game tomorrow."

It wasn't a good idea to bust their star the night before the game.

"I guess he should've thought of that," I said.

He smiled. "You should've seen him when he recognised me. I used to sweep out the mall at night, remember? He used to hang around the sports shop out there when he was a freshman. He always looked at me like I was something he scraped off his shoes. I remember one night he grabbed a paperback from my back pocket and started tossin' it back and forth like a football with this other jock. I got so mad I grabbed him by his shirt and accidentally tore it. He really beat the crap out of me. Not like you, I mean not any stitches or anything, but he really nailed me. When he was being booked tonight, he finally figured out who I was. This little computer nerd he used to push around out at the mall. He couldn't believe it."

I touched my aching head. "Maybe it was worth it."

"Maybe what was worth it?"

"Getting the crap kicked out of me."

"Yeah?"

"She wants to start going out with me."

He was stunned. No doubt about it. "The girl?"

"Right. Cindy."

"Go out with you?"

I was grinning. "Can you believe it? But that's what she said."

"God."

I wasn't sure what I was seeing or hearing at first, but then I realised he was jealous. He really had been smitten. Apparently he had his dreams of taking her out himself. She had just turned eighteen, and was perfectly legal even if she did have a semester to go before graduating high school.

"That's great," he said, but obviously didn't mean it.

I was still curious about something he'd said earlier. "So what kind of other trouble is Myles in?"

"I really can't talk about it. just an idea of my own I've had. Haven't even told the Chief about it."

I felt sorry for him, then.

He was all puffed up in his uniform tonight, and he'd met the kind of girl dweebs like us always dreamed about and tried so uselessly to possess, and then I went and spoiled it for him.

"I rented the second Conan movie the other night," I said. "I think I like it better than the first one. You know, where Arnold gets drunk and loses the girl he's supposed to be guarding. It's really funny."

"Yeah," he said. But he wasn't listening. I had the sense he was thinking about Cindy.

A knock.

He went to the door and opened it. I couldn't see who was

there but I saw his whole body tense and then he said, "Come in."

She'd changed into a white sweater and a blue jacket styled like a Navy pea jacket. Her hair was combed straight back, almost like a mane, and the deep red natural colour of her lips made me want to kiss her.

She came right over to me and picked up my hand and gave it a squeeze and then leaned in and carefully gave me a kiss on the cheek.

"You're going to be fine," she said.

"That's what I hear."

"He's such an asshole. Pardon my French."

"I guess I couldn't disagree with you there."

"It's all my fault."

"Don't be ridiculous."

"It really is, and you know it."

"God, Cindy, he just needed to explode and he picked whoever was around. It's his fault, not anybody else's."

"Well, I called your parents and apologised, anyway. Your dad said he'd come down and get you, but I said I'd give you a ride home."

I felt that old flattery again.

Girl like Cindy Brasher offering to give me a ride home. And in front of a witness.

I knew it probably made Garrett jealous and angry to hear all this but I didn't care. In a mean way, in fact, I probably enjoyed it a little bit. His uniform had made him a big man. Cindy Brasher's interest in me was making me a big man, too. That's the thing I figured out about love a long time ago. It's not how your lover feels about you that matters — it's how your lover makes you feel about yourself that counts.

"Sorry to spoil your fun, Miss Brasher," Garrett said, "but I'm afraid he'll have to ride home with me."

"With you?" she said, sounding genuinely disappointed.

"Afraid so."

"But why?"

"I've still got some questions to ask him. About what happened tonight, I mean."

I saw what he was doing. The pettiness of it was so pathetic it was almost laughable. Revenge of the Conan Readers.

She looked angry.

I took her hand.

"I'll call you tomorrow," I said.

She continued to glare at Garrett.

"No, you won't," she said. "I'll call you. As soon as I get up."

She gave me another cautious kiss on the cheek, scowled again at Garrett, and left.

The squad car smelled of puke and disinfectant and cold, cold night. Cops hauled a lot of drunks.

After he pulled out of the hospital parking lot, Garrett said, "You going to press charges?"

"Sure. Why wouldn't I?"

"'For the good of the cause' as the Mayor put it to me."

"You're shitting me. The Mayor doesn't want me to press charges?"

"That's the idea he gave me."

"Well, fuck him."

He looked over at me solemnly. "What if I told you that I was going to nail him on a couple of charges a lot worse than assault and battery?"

"A lot worse?"

"Uh-huh."

"Man, you just started working tonight. How could you have anything on him?"

"Yeah, but I've been following some things very closely. That's one thing they taught us at the Academy. To watch things that don't seem to be related."

"Like what?"

57

He didn't say anything for a time. Just drove. His uniform gave him the right to be mysterious.

The mercury vapour lights made the glowing snow purple. No other cars were on the street. The town looked doomed.

"You been following the robberies?"

"What robberies?" I said.

"Eight convenience stores in little towns all within fifteen miles east and west of here."

"Guess not." Of course not. Why would I follow anything like that?

The radio squawked. He picked it up and checked in and then ten-foured.

He looked over at me and grinned. "I do that shit pretty good, don't I?"

"Yeah, Conan couldn't have done it any better."

He laughed. "That'd make a great movie. You know, fish-out-of-water. Conan gets transported forward in time and is a cop."

It really was a pretty funny idea.

Then, "Three weeks ago, in one of the robberies, two store clerks got murdered."

"That's right. I forgot about that." Then, realising his implication, I said, "God, you think Myles had something to do with that?"

"Maybe. But if you tell anybody, I'll deny I said it."

"Why would he rob convenience stores? His old man's rich and he's a football hero."

"Have some fun, maybe. Who knows?"

"Anyway, how could you tie him to it?"

"Hamstring."

"Huh?"

He shook his head. "Maybe I'll explain someday."

He pulled up in front of my house. All the lights were on. Mom and Dad and Josh would be waiting up. Nervously.

Just as I was getting out of the car, I said, "You could've let her drive me home."

"I know. But I figure the less time she spends with you, the better my chances are."

At least he was finally being honest about it.

"Man, who would've thought that two comic book nerds like us would be going after the same beautiful girl?" I suppose I felt sorry for him again. At the moment I felt that Cindy was completely mine. I could afford to joke with him.

"Too bad she doesn't have a twin," he said, and then put the car into gear.

"Yeah," I said, "too bad."

And then I closed the door.

And then he was gone.

Richard Mitchell, KNAX-TV:

"Another problem they had with the last execution here at the prison was that one member of the execution team snuck in a tiny camera to the death chamber and secretly snapped pictures of the prisoner while he was dying. He then sold the photos to one of the tabloid TV shows for a lot of money. So tonight, before the execution team enters the chamber, every member is going to be searched. The warden doesn't want a repeat of last time."

Tape 21-D, August 14. Interview between Attorney Risa Wiggins and her client in the Clark County jail.

A: The alien was controlling your mind?

C: Absolutely.

A: Tell me about the headaches again.

C: You mean the ones I got right before it would take control of me again?

A: Yes.

C: Well, I'd see it for what it was. I'd have these blinding pains in my head and then I'd see the alien, what it really looked like, I mean. It was horrifying.

A: You do admit that you took LSD a few times several years ago?

C: Yes.

A: Could all of this have been some kind of flashback?

C: No way, no.

9

It was sort of like being sick when you were a little kid. Everybody was extra nice to you.

I spent the next morning sitting in the living room watching *Repo Man*, one of my favourite science fiction movies, and sipping the honey-laced tea my mom made for me.

Josh came home for lunch from school, something he didn't do very often. He brought me a paperback he thought I might like. Josh didn't know anything about science fiction but he had heard the name Heinlein. *The Door Into Summer*, the book he'd bought me, just happened to be one I hadn't read in a long time. It was a great book. I hated to call anything 'sweet' but that's just what the book was.

By now, the headache was pretty much gone. The stitches still hurt, and I was moving pretty slowly, but I felt much better than I had when Garrett dropped me off last night.

Dad came home for lunch, too.

He handed me an envelope. Inside was a cheque for twenty-five dollars.

"You don't need to do this," I said. My parents weren't exactly rich.

"I should've done a lot more when you were a little kid."

"You sure?"

"Sure I'm sure." He smiled. "Spend it on that Brasher girl."

"Thanks, Dad."

Josh spent a few minutes with me before he left. "You're the big news at school."

"I am?" I said.

"Sure. You broke Cindy and Myles up for one thing."

"They were already breaking up."

"Yeah, but you look like a heartbreaker."

"I'm not even sure what a 'heartbreaker' is."

He grinned. "A heartbreaker is a stud."

"Yeah, that's me all right. A stud."

"And people are saying that it's also very cool that you're not pressing charges."

"I'm not?"

"Judge Sweeney will arraign him on Monday for the traffic violations, but will let him play today since you're not pressing charges. People're saying it's cool that you put the school's interest before your own. Those are the exact words our esteemed class president said to me. 'It's cool that your brother is putting the school's interest before his own.' Then he said something else but I probably better not tell you what that was."

"Now you *have* you tell me what it was."

He smiled. He loved baiting me. Gave him a sense of power. Picking on me that way.

"He said, 'You know, it's funny. I guess I always thought your brother was sort of a dipshit, but I guess I was wrong about him.'"

I suppose it should have hurt my feelings but I laughed. There was an innocence about it that was funny.

"Tell him I still am a dipshit."

"Yeah," Josh said, rallying to my defence, "but you're not as big a dipshit as you *used* to be."

"Boy, that's comforting to know."

"Anyway, thanks for not pressing charges. We couldn't win the game if Myles didn't play."

I hadn't officially been asked to press charges anyway, but I figured I may as well play the forgiving hero. Now that I wasn't as big a dipshit as I used to be, I had to start doing noble stuff like that.

Around one, the house settled down again, Josh and Dad back to school and work respectively, Mom off for her Friday afternoon grocery shopping.

I watched an episode of *Land of the Giants* on the Sci-Fi Channel. The first act was so bad it was good, but the second act was so bad it was just plain awful. I switched over to the beginning of *High Plains Drifter*, which is just about my favourite western because of the fantasy element, and I stayed with it through the first thirty-six killings, and then I kind of dozed off, I guess. They'd given me some extra pain medication to take home last night. The stuff made me groggy.

At first, I thought the phone was part of the dream I was having. In the dream, I was getting this call I knew to be urgent but every time I reached out to pick up the receiver, the phone moved away from me, further and further away until I knew I'd never be able to reach it, even though it was like this life-and-death call.

Then I woke up and grabbed the phone in reality.

"Hello."

"You fucking go out with her, man, I'm going to fucking kill you. You fucking understand me?"

Apparently he'd been told to use 'fucking' in every sentence he spoke today.

I hung up.

He called back.

"Last night was just the warm-up, asshole."

"I'm not pressing charges, jerk-off. I'm doing you a favour."

"I don't give a shit if you press charges or not. All I give a shit about is Cindy."

"That's between you two."

"I want you to leave her alone."

I was scared, then I was angry, then, and this kind of surprised me, I was a little bit sad. For Myles, I mean. He was a bully and all but he was in great pain right now – in his way, I guessed he probably did love Cindy – and he didn't know what to do with it. All he could do was get angry, but he sensed that wouldn't get Cindy back. And that just made him angrier than ever. If that makes sense.

"Maybe you could try being nice to Cindy," I said.

"Don't give me any of your faggot bullshit, Spencer."

"I'm going to hang up, Myles. And I don't want you to call

me any more. All right?"

"You faggot, you see her one more time and I'll kill you. You fucking understand me?"

He was the one who hung up.

10

At first I wasn't sure I liked the idea of the roses. I mean, roses aren't something you send a he-man, even one who used to be something of a dipshit.

But after my mom got them in the vase and sitting up on the table in front of the window... they looked very pretty... especially now that the snow had stopped and the sun was out and the afternoon had warmed all the way up to thirty-four.

"I wonder who sent them."

"Probably Cindy," I said.

"Well, wasn't that nice of her?" Mom said. "She sure sounds like a nice girl."

"Yeah, she is." And then I closed my eyes and pictured her a moment. And then I said again, "Yeah, she is."

"I wasn't sure if you'd like them."

"They're great."

"Your mom fixed them up so nice."

"Yeah."

"I really like your parents."

"They really like you."

"Really? They said that?"

I smiled. "Really. They said that."

Mom and Dad had gone to a movie at the Cineplex. Josh had gone to the game. They'd all been there when Cindy had shown up. It was kind of awkward at first, me never having exactly had a girlfriend before, but then everybody got along great.

"When did they say it?" Cindy said.

"When did they say what?"

"That they liked me?"

"Oh. Right before they left."

"I didn't hear them say anything."

"They whispered it."

"You're not making it up?"

"Huh-uh."

For a beautiful, bright girl, Cindy had almost as many insecurities as I did.

We were on the couch. She'd already given me eight or nine kisses so I wasn't nervous about kissing her back. I took her face to mine and gave her a kiss and it was like a contact high.

"There's a David Cronenberg movie on in twenty minutes."

"David Cronenberg?"

"He's a director. Canadian."

"Oh."

"It's a little bit gross."

"What's it called?"

"*The Brood.*"

"What's it about?"

"These little babies that are monsters."

"Do they look real, you know, icky and stuff?"

"Pretty icky."

"Do you have any Barbara Streisand movies?"

"Huh-uh."

"Maybe there'll be something on MTV."

"Yeah, maybe."

She made popcorn and we watched MTV. It was the usual stuff. The VJ named Kennedy kept trying to make a fool of herself and pretty much succeeded; and a couple of rap songs talked about what pigs girls were and how white guys pretty much deserved to die; and then one of the MTV male-model types came on and traded a few yuks with Kennedy and pretended that he was pretty much like all the guys watching the show, except maybe for his Porsche convertible and the $10,000 worth of caps on his teeth.

After MTV there was this show called *Dimension 4*, which was about all these allegedly true stories of people who have been abducted, and who have paranormal powers, and who claim they can channel the voices of people who used to live in condos in Atlantis.

I started mocking some of the guests and for the first time, Cindy got irritated with me.

"That's not very nice."

"Cindy, the guy claimed that the alien gives him extra sexual powers and that he'd like to hear from a bunch of women so he could demonstrate how good he is these days."

"So?"

"Doesn't that sound like a put-on?"

"Gee, the way you like science fiction, I'd think you'd have more of an open mind."

I saw that it really was bothering her, the way I'd made fun of the people, and then I realised that I'd slipped back into my dipshit mode. Putting people down. Sounding like Mr Know-It-All on the *Bullwinkle* show.

"Hey, I'm sorry, I really am."

"I believe in aliens, she said.

"You do?"

I couldn't help it. When she said that, my mind immediately went back to the breakdown she'd had, and the time she'd spent in the mental hospital.

"Yes, I do." She looked distant a moment, as if she was remembering something painful. "In fact, I know someone whose mind has been taken over by an alien."

"You do?"

"Yes. And you know him, too."

"I do?"

She nodded. "There's a well out in the woods."

"A well?"

"I'd like to take you there. Would you go?"

"Sure," I said. But I was thinking about her breakdown

and the mental hospital again.

For a moment there, I had the suspicion that she was putting me on. Then I realised that it wasn't her style, being sly like that. For all her beauty, she was nervous a lot of the time, and spoke in a very straightforward way. The put-on wasn't part of her.

I was going to say more but that was when I saw headlights sweep the front windows, and heard a car pull into the driveway.

"My folks," I said.

She looked at the clock. "Gosh, it's after ten already."

"That's not very late."

"For you it is," she said. "You need your rest. That's the only way you're going to get better."

"I'm already better."

I tugged her face gently to mine. "Especially after tonight." This was our first French kiss.

I wanted to start running around the room and yelling yippee the way Yosemite Sam might have but I decided that that was something only a dipshit would do.

Instead I said, "I really like you, Cindy."

And she just looked at me and I couldn't read her.

And I was scared because I knew she could break my heart any time she wanted to, utterly destroy me. When somebody has that kind of power over you, you're a fool not to fear them in some ways.

"I really do know somebody who's being controlled by an alien," she said very softly. "When you're better, I want to take you someplace, OK?"

"I'd love to go."

I was afraid she wasn't ever going to say anything romantic back to me.

Then she smiled and said, "I really like you, too. I just wanted you to know that."

Then my folks were there, and the fun was all over.

11

Two nights later, we went to get a pizza, and afterward she took me out to the well.

Everything was silent except for our feet crunching through the layer of ice. The town spread out below us like a mirage on a vast white prairie. A midnight train ran the length of the distant countryside, tearing through the darkness with purpose and fury.

The moonlight on the snow gave the woods a soft glow. Fox and possum and raccoon and rabbit darted through the undergrowth as we made our way deeper into the stands of hardwoods. My nose and cheeks were frozen. Our breath was vapour. Despite the cold, every time I'd touch her for any significant time, I'd get an erection. I was a virgin, but not a happy one.

Little kids in our town believe that there are two long-haunted places. One is the old red brick school abandoned back in the fifties. The story they tell is that there was this really wicked principal, a warted crone who looked a lot like Miss Grundy in *Archie* comics, who on two occasions took two different first-graders to the basement and beat them so badly that they died. Legend has it that she cracked the concrete floor, buried them beneath it and poured fresh concrete. Legend also has it that even today the spirits of those two little kids still haunt the old schoolhouse and that, on certain nights, the ghost of the principal can be seen carrying a blood-dripping axe.

The other legend concerns Parkinson's cabin, a place built in the mid-1800s by a white man who planned to do a lot of business with the Mesquakie Indians. Except something went wrong. The local newspaper noted that a huge meteor was seen by many locals one night, and that it crashed to earth not far from Trapper Parkinson's crude cabin. The odd thing was, nobody ever saw or talked to Parkinson again after the meteor crash. Perfect soil for a legend to grow.

It took us thirty-five minutes to reach the cabin from the road. About halfway there, Cindy finally told me that that was where we were headed. Bramble and first-growth pine made the last of our passage slow. But then we stood on a small hill, the moon big and round and blanched white like the one the Aztec priests always called a demon moon, and looked down on a disintegrating lean-to of boards and tar paper. Over the years, hobos had periodically tried to fix the place up. An ancient plough, all blade-rusted and wood-rotted, stood next to the cabin. A silver snake of moon-touched creek ran behind.

And then Cindy said, "You see it over there? The well?"

Sometime in the early part of this century, when the last of the Mormons were trekking their way across the country to Utah, a straggling band stopped here long enough to help a young couple finish the well they'd started digging. The Mormons, being decent folks indeed, even built the people a pit made of native stone and a roof made of birch. And the well itself hadn't been easy to dig. You started with a sharp-pointed augur looking for water and then you dug with a shovel when you found it. Sometimes you dug two hundred feet, sending up buckets of rock and dirt and shale for days before you were done. It was all tumbledown now, of course, but you could see in the remnants of the pit how impressive it must have been when it was new.

We went over to the well. Cindy ducked beneath the shabby roof and peered straight down into the darkness. I dropped a rock down there. The rock broke a thin skin of ice. The echoes rose. I shone my light down. This was what they call a dug well, about the only kind most people made back then. Most of the dug wells in this area went down into clay and shale about fifty feet.

I kept my light trained down there.

"He probably doesn't like the light."

I looked up at her. "Who doesn't like the light?"

71

"I guess I shouldn't say 'he.' I should say 'it.'"

"I guess I'm not following you, Cindy."

She sighed and walked a few feet away from the well. I didn't go after her. Right now, for some reason, I didn't want to touch her. It was almost as if I was afraid to touch her.

There was white moonlit snow and there was deep prairie shadow around the cabin, and on a smaller hill nearby there were deer.

But mostly there was just the wind whipping up snow crystals, and the silence. There was a whole lot of silence.

"You'll just laugh at me if I tell you," she said. She sounded almost angry.

"No, I won't."

"You know I had a breakdown. Everybody in this whole fucking town knows I had a breakdown."

"I won't laugh at you, Cindy. I promise."

She didn't speak, didn't move, for maybe half a minute, and then she walked back over to me and said, "You really promise?"

"I really promise."

"I can't stand it when people laugh at me. That's what it was like when I came back from the hospital. I'd walk by people and I could hear them whispering and see them smirking. And I'd tell this to my so-called shrink and he'd just say I was being paranoid. He also tried putting the moves on me, the asshole."

"Your shrink?"

"Yeah. I really hated him."

"Why didn't you tell somebody?"

She glared at me. "Why didn't I tell somebody? Because I was crazy and if I told anybody they'd just see that as proof that I was crazy. Dr Granger is an important man in this town." She shook her head. "But I don't give a shit about that. It's the well I want to tell you about."

"And I want to hear it."

She walked over to the fieldstone edge of the well and looked down inside.

"He's some kind of space alien."

I didn't say anything.

"He was inside the meteor that crashed here that time."

"And he stays down in the well?"

"Yes."

"Why?"

"Because if humans ever laid eyes on him, they'd go insane. Right on the spot."

How do you know that?"

"I – communicate with him."

"I see."

She glanced up at me. "You don't believe me, do you?"

"I'm listening, Cindy. With an open mind. I really am."

"You think space aliens exist?"

"I think it's possible."

"You think one could exist down this well?"

"I think that's possible, too."

"You're not just saying that?"

"No."

"Really?"

"Really."

"Good," she said.

"How did you find out about it?" I said.

"That's the part I can't tell you."

"Why not?"

"Because I'd get my friend in trouble. My ex-friend, guess."

As soon as she said ex-friend, I suspected who she was talking about.

"David Myles told you about the alien, didn't he?"

"I really can't talk about that part of it. I hate him, but I don't want to get him in trouble."

I thought of what Garrett had hinted at, that he thought Myles was in some serious trouble.

"We did things," she said.

She spoke so softly, I could barely hear.

73

At first, I assumed she was talking about sexual relationships. Maybe now that they'd broken up she regretted sleeping with him.

But then she said, "He did the things. But I was there. I didn't stop him."

Then: "Put your head down into the well a little."

"Like this?" I said.

"Yeah."

I kept my head down there for a full minute. The wind whined as it whipped in circles inside the well.

"You hear anything?" she said.

"Just the wind."

"Listen harder."

I knew what she wanted me to hear. And I wanted to hear it, too.

But I didn't hear anything.

When I brought my head up, I saw her watching me, disappointed.

"Maybe it takes a couple of times," she said.

"I'm willing to try it again sometime."

"You're just so damned good to me."

She came over to me then and pulled me to her. She kissed me with a kind of desperation that alarmed me a little.

And then we were making love.

It was crazy, it was so cold, and there really wasn't even any good place to lean against.

But she was slipping her jeans down. She got one leg of them off entirely so that I could put myself up inside her.

And then we were doing it, her leaning back against the well, and finding the rhythm and the moisture to pull me up way deep inside her. Her thighs were cold but her sex was so hot and nurturing that it warmed my entire body.

She had a wonderful body and she really knew what she was doing.

I just kind of followed her lead. When she went fast, I went fast. When she slowed down, I slowed down.

One time something funny happened, I heard this voice, it was very strange, it wasn't hers, it wasn't mine, it wasn't even out loud, at least I don't think it was. It was just this voice in my head, and it said something that I couldn't understand, I couldn't understand at all. I thought maybe it was the wind — out here on the prairie, the wind gets pretty strange sometimes.

But mostly I just gave myself over to making love to Cindy.

There was passion, but there was tenderness, too. That was the part I liked.

She'd pause every once in a while and hold my face between her hands and look at me and say, "I'm really falling in love with you."

And then we'd start up again.

I held on as long as I could.

Every time I thought I was going to come, I'd slow down so I could hold out longer.

But then I couldn't help myself and I said, "I'm going to come," and she said "Oh, yes; yes yes," and I came and it was sort of like dying, I don't know how else to describe it, it was like I was surrendering my entire being to her, and I wanted to, I wanted her to take me and control me the rest of my life.

And then we were done, spent.

I got down on my haunches and helped get the leg of her jeans back on. I couldn't help myself from touching her there again. I felt where I'd just been, felt where we commingled, and she must have sensed what I was feeling because she put her hand on mine and left it there for a long and tender moment.

On the way back to town, her driving her dad's nice new car, she said, "I wish you would've heard it."

"Maybe I did."

"God, really?"

I told her about the strange brief muffled words in my head as we'd been making love.

"That's how it was the first time for me, too," she said.

Then we were quiet for a time, there was just the heater blowing and a rock ballad playing, and the farm fields blue in the midnight moon ran on and on, flat and beautiful, for endless miles.

"I want to tell you something," I said.

She looked at me curiously. "All right."

"I was a virgin until tonight."

She smiled. "God, I wish I could say the same."

"I mean, you didn't guess?"

"Huh-uh. You did just fine."

I could feel myself grinning. Couldn't help it. "I was afraid I'd do something stupid."

"Like what?"

"Oh, I don't know. Come too fast or something like that."

"You did just great. Really. Just great."

Then she reached over and took my hand and gave it a quick squeeze. "I really am falling in love with you."

"I'm falling in love with you, too."

"I know," she smiled. "And that's what makes it so nice."

12

Summer came the following week.

That's a local joke, about how you can have summer and winter and summer again all within the same month. Sometimes within the same week.

But it really was sort of like summer, people walking around downtown in their shirtsleeves and dresses.

By noon, the temperature was in the seventies and the sunlight was very warm. Convertible tops went down and everywhere you went you heard loud rock and roll music. It was like the town was having this party.

On my lunch hour, I walked over to Taubman's Cigar Store. That's what it's always been called, but even though they sell cigarettes and cigars it's mostly a newsstand where I buy all my science fiction paperbacks.

The big thing at Taubman's is the skin magazines. Two or three times in the past few years, The Women Of Righteousness picketed the place, but Mr Taubman didn't give in.

Mr Taubman keeps the skin magazines in the back of his store, so that's where you usually find the crowd. It's always kind of fun to watch guys go back there. Some of them look kind of sneaky and furtive. Some kind of swagger, as if they're daring you to say anything about what they're doing. And some are just fast, shoot back there, thumb through a few pages, and then shoot back out into the street.

I spent twenty minutes going through the new paperbacks. I bought two of them, a Koontz and a King, them pretty much being my favourite writers.

I was just leaving when I saw Garrett coming through the doorway.

Even though his shift didn't start for a couple of hours, he was already in uniform.

Any self-consciousness he'd had those first few days was already gone.

When he saw me, he paused in the doorway, nodded for me to follow, and then turned around and walked back outside.

He said hello to a couple of passing people, and then gave a long, hard look to a very pretty young mother pushing her baby in his stroller down the block. She had beautiful ankles.

He didn't say anything to me, just started walking, and I fell in next to him.

It was kind of strange, neither of us saying anything, just walking. We passed the Lutheran church with its towering spire; and the First Trust bank building where, according to legend, John Dillinger stopped one day while fleeing federal agents; and the Orpheum theatre that closed down after the four-plex went up in the mall.

Then we reached the city park, and it was all pretty women, and little kids playing Frisbee with dogs, and old men on park benches, and motorboats out on the river.

"You eat yet?" Garrett said.

"Huh-uh."

"You want a hot dog?"

"Yeah, OK."

There was a small concrete block concession stand. We got two Pepsis and two chili dogs and went over and sat on a bench by the river.

I could tell he wanted to say something.

He said, "Guess what I read this weekend?"

"What?"

"Four of those old Roy Thomas Conan comic books."

"Wow, I haven't seen those since I was a kid."

"They were really good."

But that wasn't what he really wanted to say. That was just talk. Nervous talk.

He said, "Went on my first drug bust last night."

"Yeah?"

"Yeah. I was scared shitless. The Captain said that these guys would be armed. You know, dealers."

"Were they?"

"Yeah, they were. One of them even had a sawed-off shotgun. Lucky for us, they were stoned out of their fucking minds. All we had to do was waltz in there and bust the bastards."

He was already a cop. With the attitude, I mean, and hard edge. He'd only been wearing the uniform about three weeks.

But the drug bust wasn't what he wanted to tell me about, either.

We sat in silence a little longer and the little kids laughing and toddling around on the grass was kind of fun to watch.

He said, "He's a big hero."

"Who is?"

"Myles."

"Oh."

"You didn't press charges so he could play that game and he goes and scores more points than he ever has and we win the conference championship so now he's king shit again instead of this creep who beat you up."

"Well, I got something good out of it." I looked over at him and smiled. "Cindy."

We watched each other for a moment and then looked back at the river. Sometimes it's easy to imagine the days when the big paddle-wheelers plied this river and unloaded supplies here on the shore. The old-timers say that Indians used to run for miles on the shore right along with the paddle-wheelers, waving and laughing the whole time.

He said, "I've got to tell you something."

Whatever he was about to say was the real thing he wanted to tell me. Not Conan, not drug busts. This.

"She's seeing him again."

"Cindy?"

"Uh-huh."

"Bullshit."

There was a sweet, soft breeze, but I couldn't enjoy it. I didn't believe what he'd told me, but somehow I didn't quite disbelieve him, either.

The fast few days, Cindy had been acting odd. The nights we went out, she found a reason to go home early. And any plans I suggested, she always put off, saying she wasn't sure what her schedule would be like.

She wouldn't even kiss me right, either.

I guess that was the worst of it because that's where I could really feel her slipping away from me, her kisses too quick, too cold.

"She hates him," I said.

"Maybe."

"And since she hates him, it wouldn't make any sense that she was seeing him, would it?"

"I just thought you should know." I was quiet for a time. Then, "Somebody tell you this or you see it for yourself?"

"I saw it for myself."

"When?"

"Last few nights."

"Where?"

"Couple of different places. Out behind McDonald's where all the kids hang out?"

"Yeah?"

"He was kissing her."

I felt a lot of things just then, but mostly I felt sick. I saw a little kid tottering across the grass in search of his fallen Frisbee. It really would be good to be a kid again and not give a damn about a girl betraying you.

He said, "She tell you anything about him?"

"Like what?"

"Anything he might have done that was against the law."

I'd forgotten his suspicions about David Myles.

"She hinted at a couple of things, I guess."

"Like what?"

"Nothing specific."

"She ever mention the Franson woman?"

"The old lady who got murdered?"

"Yeah, murdered and robbed. Her."

"No, she never mentioned her. You don't think Myles had anything to do with the Franson woman, do you?"

He shot his sleeve and looked at his wristwatch. It was silver and new and impressive. I guessed his folks gave it to him as a gift.

"I'm not sure yet."

He stood up and I saw it in him, too, the way I'd seen it in my younger brother Josh. Garrett the cop here was becoming an adult. We were the same age and I was still a boy and he was becoming an adult.

Then I remembered the well and said, "She's got this weird thing about a well."

"What kind of well?"

I told him.

"You know she was in the mental hospital, don't you?"

"Yeah."

"Now I can see why."

I should have defended her, but I was too angry. I had no doubt that Garrett had told me the truth about Myles kissing her. I wanted somebody to dislike Myles as much as I did. Garrett seemed willing to take on the role.

He checked his wristwatch again. "I'd better get going."

His Sam Browne creaked; his Magnum was as imposing as ever.

"You headed back to work?" he said.

"Yeah. Different direction. If you're headed to the station, I mean."

He smiled. "Yeah' I'm at the stage where I hang around there even when I'm not on duty. The older cops tell me I'll get over that fast."

I nodded. "Thanks for telling me about Myles."

"It's a hell of thing to have to tell somebody."

"I'd rather know than not know."

"He's got some kind of hold on her, that's for sure." Then: "You see that new SF movie that opened last weekend?"

"I wanted to. But Cindy said it looked too scary. She hates scary stuff."

Except for a well that has an alien in it, I thought unkindly.

"I've got Sunday afternoon off. If you're free, give me a call."

I put out my hand and we shook. I needed a friend very badly at the moment.

"You'll get over it," he said. "I got dumped once."

"Yeah?"

"Yeah. This little car hop out at the A&W on old 49?"

"Jeeze, I'd forgotten all about that place." Back in my high school days, that had been the sort of unofficial hangout of the dweebs and nerds. We were far enough out of town that nobody could hassle us. Plus they let us use the cigarette machine even though we were underage.

"Took me a year to get over her, but I did."

"How come she dumped you?"

He tapped his nose. "She got in this fucking car wreck."

"And that's why she dumped you?"

"Nah. She got in this car wreck and had to have all this plastic surgery on her face."

"Yeah?"

"Yeah. And the surgery turned her into a real beauty. God, she was beautiful. You should've seen her." He shrugged. "Well, anybody who looks like she did sure doesn't want to hang around somebody like me. So she dumped me. Started going out with this really handsome rich kid." He smiled. It was not without bitterness. "But she got paid back."

"How?"

"The handsome rich kid?"

"Uh-huh."

"He turned out to be a peeper."

"A peeper?"

"Yeah, you know, a guy who's always peeping into ladies' johns and places like that."

I laughed. "Man, I guess she got paid back."

He smiled and cuffed me on the arm. "Just hang in there. Maybe Myles'll turn out to be a transvestite or something."

13

That night I followed her. That's not a nice thing to admit about yourself, that you're the kind of guy who'd sneak around after your girlfriend, like the kind of guy who would call people on the phone anonymously and hassle them.

But I did.

Dark came right after dinner, and when she left the house for the evening I was parked down the block,

She went to the pharmacy first, and then to the library, and then to the mall.

Then she went to the Arby's over on Foster Avenue, and that's where she found Myles.

He was there waiting for her.

I sat in the lot and watched them in the window.

When she saw him, she gave him a quick kiss on the mouth and then sat down in his booth, across from him.

I felt sick.

I had quick, frantic dreams of going in there and hauling her out here. I'd make a strong case for myself, how I was good and true and sensitive and didn't that count for something in this world? And if she needed reminding, I'd remind her of all the terrible things Myles had done to her.

I started feeling self-conscious, the way people checked me out as they went inside.

They seemed to sense that I was a pretty sleazy character, following some poor girl around, unable to take my banishment like a mature adult.

None of it made sense to me. For three or four nights there, we'd spent a lot of great hours together, her constantly telling me how happy she was to be with me instead of him... and then I felt her pulling back.

But why?

Sometimes I looked in the window where she sat and I hated her for what she'd done to me. I couldn't ever remember pain like this.

Tonight, for example, I'd gone into my room and slid out my Penthouse from underneath my mattress where my Mom couldn't find it. Sometimes, just to cut tension (and to have as good a time as you can have alone), I masturbated. But not tonight. I looked at all the naked girls who usually aroused me, and felt nothing. Nothing. Then I'd gone into the basement where I have four small bookcases packed with science fiction paperbacks and magazines from high school. Sometimes, when I'm down, I can go down there and look at them and touch them and feel the kind of solace I used to, that even if I was a dweeb and isolated and scared, I could always hide between the covers of those books and magazines, that there was escape and mercy after all, if only you knew where to find it.

They stayed in Arby's an hour.

Some of the time, they looked to be having a very serious discussion. Other times, they laughed.

When they came out into the warm mid-November night, her arm was around his middle and he was giving her a squeeze.

They left her car there. She got in his.

If he found out that I was following them, he'd beat me up even worse than he had before.

But I didn't care. I followed them.

She sat close to him in the front seat. A lot of people honked at them, and they honked back. King and queen. Royalty.

The night didn't help. It was one of those smoky autumn nights that make you melancholy and restless without you knowing quite why.

They stopped at a jock shop where he tried on a couple of letter jackets. Again, I saw them through the windows. My own little TV show.

Maybe it would be better if he saw me and caught me, I

thought. Then we could at least get this over with.

When they came out of the jock shop, they stopped off at a convenience store where Myles bought a sixpack. He was underage but he was also Myles and they weren't going to refuse him, not in this town.

Myles had parked on the dark side of the store. When he came out, he set the beer in the back seat and then they started making out.

Right there.

We'd kind of done that, too, our last night together, wanted to kiss so badly that we couldn't control ourselves, and made out just about every place we went.

I felt sick again, wild with rage and embarrassment and self-pity.

I was so fascinated and repelled by what I saw that I didn't even hear him sneak up on me.

"You want to borrow my binoculars?" he said.

"Hey. How you doing?"

"Guess I should ask how you're doing?"

"Oh, pretty good."

"Right. That's why you're sitting here watching them make out."

He really was a cop, Garrett. He'd easily figured out what I was doing here.

"You must like punishment."

"Yeah, I must."

"Why don't you go have a beer?"

I could tell that this wasn't a suggestion, it was a subtle but definite order.

This was Garrett the cop talking, saying that it wasn't a real good situation when one citizen sat there spying on another.

"Yeah, that's probably a good idea."

He looked at me and smiled. "You'll get over it."

"Yeah, I suppose I will."

"You'll meet somebody else."

Once again, I had the sense that Garrett had become a real adult while I had remained a child. He wouldn't sit here watching her like this. He was too proud, too sensible, too much of an adult.

"I hope it's soon, Garrett."

He nodded, and then walked back to his car.

I did what he wanted me to. I fired up the beast, which was running again after smashing into Cindy's tree, and then I drove away from there – all the way around the block.

Garrett was gone.

Myles and Cindy were just pulling out.

I followed them.

14

At first I wasn't sure where they were going.

We drove out of town on an old highway that parallelled the Interstate. Everything got dark. I stayed a half mile behind. Farmhouses shone in tonight's red harvest moon. I had the window down and I could hear cows and horses and barn owls.

When he turned west, I knew where he was going to take us.

I had to smile when I tried to imagine him at the well. This hard, unimaginative football hero trying to play along with her fantasy.

Maybe that would drive her back to me, the way I'd been sympathetic and pretended that I'd heard something.

Suggestible is what I'd been.

I'd gotten caught up in her mood and then, while we were making love, my mind had started imagining the voice. At least the voice had been speaking gibberish.

I smelled hay and cow manure and silo corn and prairie night; I saw hill and creek and railroad tracks shining in the moonlight.

And then we were pulling off the road, and he was parking, and they were walking up the hill to the woods that would lead them to the shack and the well.

I gave them a ten minute start on me, and then I was out of the car and walking toward the woods.

It was spookier than I'd thought it would be.

Monsters didn't bother me. But killers did. You weren't safe anywhere these days. Just last year there'd been a guy in the adjacent county who'd kidnapped an eleven year old girl and chopped her up and ate her.

By the time I reached the end of the woods, they were already down by the cabin.

I couldn't tell what they were saying but their words were harsh and angry.

He shoved her, and then he hit her.

I could see it all clearly in the moonlight.

She sank to her knees, touching her jaw where he'd slammed his fist into her moments before.

Their words continued harsh and loud but I still couldn't quite understand them.

I wanted to go down there but I knew better. She might appreciate the fact that I saved her from him but she'd never forgive me for following them in the first place.

And then she was on her feet, and pushing him. I was surprised at her strength, surprised that he didn't hit her again.

The first time the spasm took him, he was a few feet from the well.

My first impression was that he was joking. I've seen boys try to scare their girlfriends by throwing themselves to the ground and pretending that they're having some sort of seizure.

That's what this looked like.

He started doing a sort of dance, his arms fluttering crazily in the air, his torso snapping and jerking as if in rhythm to violent music.

Then he screamed.

That's when I knew for sure that he wasn't kidding.

The spasms got even more violent over the next few minutes, and so did the screaming.

She just watched.

Didn't try to stop him or comfort him in any way.

As if she knew what was happening here and had just decided to let it run its course.

He fell to his hands and knees and, in silhouette against the blood red harvest moon, he resembled an animal, a wolf maybe, there on the ground by the well.

And then he began sobbing.

This was worse than his screaming, the way it frightened and moved me.

In the Army, I saw a man go berserk after he'd learned that

his wife had left him. He took a straight razor to his wrists in the shower. We found him huddled in the corner, beneath the water, weeping.

Myles reminded me of that forlorn man – only Myles sounded much sadder and more desperate, more primal and animal-like.

She got him to his feet somehow, and then she took him to her as if he were her child rather than her lover.

And the odd thing was, I didn't feel my usual jealousy now, seeing him in her arms this way.

For the moment anyway, I wanted her to soothe and succour him. I was being selfish. I couldn't take hearing any more of his strange wailing.

Gradually, his sobbing began to wane but still she held him, even rocking him back and forth a little, gently, gently, once again as if she were the mother and he the child.

It ended then as abruptly as it began. Myles looked spent and dropped to the ground on his knees. There was nothing more to see – or nothing more I cared to see anyway.

Had something in the well set Myles off? Or was he simply caught up in her mood as I'd been when I imagined the voices.

I laughed out loud.

Certainly, it had been nothing in the well. There was nothing in the well but water, and dirty, undrinkable water at that.

So he'd been more imaginative than I'd given him credit for – so imaginative that he fell victim to himself – imagined that something had possessed him, and overwhelmed him.

But his cries had been pretty convincing.

Damned convincing.

I was glad to be out of the woods, and in my car, and heading back home.

Popcorn and Pepsi and *Late Night With David Letterman* sounded damned good about now.

15

But they didn't work for me, neither popcorn nor David Letterman.

I sat on the moonlit screened-in back porch. It was mild as a spring night and it was November. I wanted to be a kid again. I wanted to be anybody but who I was at that moment.

I thought about her and how I'd never be able to love anybody ever again the way I loved her. My first affair and it had lasted all of a week.

There had been a basketball game tonight. I should have gone to that, seen Josh play. It was heading to midnight now. He was likely out with his girlfriend.

A weariness overcame me. I felt a kind of paralysis. The night air was so sweet and sentimental, I didn't want to go inside.

I put my head back and closed my eyes.

I tasted her, tasted her mouth, tasted her sex. I didn't think I'd done especially well at oral sex — I really was a virgin — despite her claims that I'd been "wonderful."

A car pulled into the driveway, headlights illuminating the closed white garage door. Josh.

He put the car away, shut up the garage, and walked up on the back porch.

"How's it going, Romeo?"

That's what he'd started calling me after he found out I was taking Cindy out.

He sat in the chair next to mine.

"You shouldn't call me that anymore."

"No? How come?"

"She dumped me."

"Dumped you? Shit, you've only had about four or five dates with her." He grinned. "Nobody could get sick of you that fast."

I had to smile, though it was painful. "She went back with

Myles."

"You're kidding. He beat her up all the time."

"I know."

"You sure about that?"

"I saw them together. And Garrett told me."

"Garrett the cop?"

"Yeah," I said.

"No offence, but when I was a little kid and he was always hanging around here – I thought he was the biggest dweeb of all."

"Yeah, I guess I did, too."

"And he grows up to be a cop." He grinned again. "I saw him strutting around downtown in his uniform yesterday. Always got his hand on the butt of his pistol. Like a western gunfighter."

"Yeah, I noticed that."

He stuck out his very long legs.

"Give her a call tomorrow," he said.

"Who?"

"Who? Cindy."

"Call her?"

"Damned right call her. Tell her it's Saturday and you want to meet her downtown on your lunch hour. No offence, Romeo, but you've got to be forceful with women."

Once again, it was little brother giving big brother advice.

"It's pretty embarrassing sometimes," I said.

"Look, brother, one thing you've got to understand about women. They like it when you embarrass yourself over them. That way they know you care about them. Maybe that's all it'll take."

"Just calling her?"

"Yeah, and showing that you really care about her." I felt a loopy exhilaration. Everything would be fine. I'd call her and after a little initial reluctance she'd be glad to hear from me and she'd agree to have lunch and when she saw me at the restaurant she wouldn't be able to help herself any more. She'd rush into my arms and things would be right between us again. The way they had been last week.

"I also got somebody to take care of Myles for you."

"You did?"

"Yeah, there's a sophomore fullback named Nick Reynolds. He can bench press 350. He's also a boxer. When he was a freshman, Myles gave him a lot of shit and Reynolds never forgot it. I was telling him about you and Myles over some brewskis the other night and he said he's been looking for a reason to punch out Myles for a long time. He says Myles gives you any more shit about Cindy, you just tell me and I'll tell Reynolds and Reynolds'll punch his face in."

"Sort of like a hit man?"

He laughed. "Yeah, kind of, I guess."

He looked at me and then did something that surprised me, leaned over and gave me a little hug. "You look like you're pretty sad, brother."

I was afraid I was going to cry. I was a wuss enough already. "Yeah, I guess I am."

"Fuck her. That's the attitude you've got to take with women. I got my heart broke in tenth grade and I'll tell you, man, never again. Now I do everything I can for them but if they want to dick me around and break my heart, I just say fuck 'em and walk away. That's all you can do. It really is."

I'd felt good for a moment there, felt that I was going to make things right with Cindy, but now I felt bad again.

I couldn't say fuck you to Cindy and walk away. I couldn't and I knew it.

"You think you'll ever get around to asking me about the game tonight, Romeo?"

"Hey, I forgot."

"I noticed."

"You win?"

"97 – 68."

"God."

"And I scored thirty-eight of them all by myself."

"Wow."

"You want to drink a brewski on that?"

"Yeah. That sounds great." I was rallying again.

"I'll steal a couple from the fridge. The old man won't mind." He stood up and walked to the kitchen door. "Remember, Romeo. What's the motto?"

"'Fuck 'em.'"

"That's right. 'Fuck 'em.'"

Yeah, I felt real good right then, and it must have lasted for all of thirty seconds.

16

"Hi, Mrs Brasher. I was just wondering if Cindy was up yet."

"I'm afraid not, Spence. Would you like her to call you?"

"No, that's all right. I'll just try her a little later."

"All right. I'll give her the message."

Mrs Brasher was always nice to me. I'd only been out there three times but each time she went out of her way to make me comfortable. With Mr Brasher it had been different. He said hello and shook hands and everything but then he didn't say anything else, just sat in his recliner and watched TV. Every once in a while I'd sense him staring at me. Sizing me up, I suppose, wondering why his daughter would trade in a football hero for somebody like me. But hadn't they noticed her black eyes and all the other bruises?

"Thanks, Mrs Brasher."

I tried half an hour later.

"Hi, Mrs Brasher. It's me again."

"Oh, hello, Spence."

This time she didn't sound quite so happy to hear from me.

"Is she –"

"– not yet, Spence. But I'd be happy to have her call you."

But what if she got the message and decided not to call me?

These were dangerous times.

"Nah, that's all right. I'll try again later."

"I wouldn't try before noon, Spence."

"All right, Mrs Brasher. I'm sorry to bother you."

I spent most of the morning driving around in my old beater. I stopped in at the used paperback place and found an old

Dan J Marlowe I hadn't read – Marlowe was a great crime writer – a novel called *Never Live Twice*. Usually, I would have been pretty excited.

But all I did was pay for it and then walk outside and drop it on the passenger seat and start driving around again.

"Hi, Mrs Brasher."

A long sigh. "Hello, Spence."

"I was wondering if –"

"I thought we agreed to twelve o'clock."

"Oh, I'm sorry, I thought you said around twelve."

My whole body was shaking. Now I'd alienated my one lone ally in the Brasher house.

"Well, even if I *had* said *around* twelve, Spence, it's only two minutes after eleven."

"Oh."

"This isn't a good way to make her want to see you, Spence."

"It isn't?"

"No. You've got to give her a little room."

"Oh."

Then: "I'm sorry, Spence. I really like you."

"Well, I really like you, too, Mrs Brasher."

Then: "She's going shopping at the mall this afternoon. Maybe you could just kind of 'accidentally' meet her there. She's supposed to meet some of her friends there around two o'clock."

"God, thanks for telling me, Mrs Brasher."

She laughed. "My pleasure, Spence – as long as you don't call back in fifteen minutes."

"I won't. I promise."

"We both like you, Spence, the mister and me. We hope she'll want to see you again. But just take it a little easy, all right?"

"Thanks, Mrs Brasher."

On weekends, the farmers come to the mall, a lot of them. It's kind of funny to think of us as 'town people' when the town's barely 25,000 but there is a difference in the way we dress and talk and even walk around the mall. I guess we all have to feel superior to somebody so we feel superior to the farmers. They just don't understand life as it's lived by big-city sophisticates like ourselves.

God basically invented malls so high school boys would have a nice dry place to hit on girls. At least that's how I see it.

This Saturday was no exception. Love and lust bloomed every three yards or so, all kinds of boys making all kinds of fools of themselves over all kinds of girls.

I got there early to check out the B Dalton. There were a couple of Roger Zelazny reprints I wanted to buy but I figured I wouldn't look real macho coming up to Cindy with a couple of books in my hand.

She wasn't there at two, and I got almost panicky. And she wasn't there are two-thirty, and I got even more panicky.

I patrolled the mall south to east, west to north.

As I'd been ever since she dumped me, I was alternatively despairing, optimistic, angry, joyous, confident, terrified.

And then I saw her.

The scariest thing in the world for most boys is to approach a girl when she's with a group of other girls. At least it is if you're as shy as I am.

But today I didn't even hesitate. I went right up to her.

A couple of her friends smirked.

Cindy herself looked nervous then faintly angry then a little bit sorry for me.

The girls kept on smirking.

They were the popular girls and to them I was the kind of guy who installed their VCRs or worked on their cars. I wasn't the kind of guy you talked to in public.

I knew I had to do what Josh had told me to.

I said, out loud and right in front of all of them, "I thought maybe you'd like to go over to Orange Julius with me."

Titters.

She looked embarrassed for both of us.

Then, one of her friends nudging her and giggling, she said, "Sure, why not?"

The nudging friend said, "Hey, you were supposed to go shopping with us."

"Go ahead," Cindy said. "I'll catch up with you later."

They all looked at me with great scorn. Then they looked at Cindy with great puzzlement.

Why would she be going over to Orange Julius with me?

"I think your mom's mad at me."

"Actually, my mom likes you."

"Yeah, but I called you a lot this morning."

"Oh, right. Well, I guess she was a little irritated. But not much."

"I really like her."

I wasn't sure what I'd actually planned to say to her but whatever it was, this wasn't it.

We sat at a small table in Orange Julius and watched all the people go by in the mall.

They all seemed infinitely happier than I would ever be, and I hated them a little bit for it.

"Boy, isn't it great out today?"

"Yeah," I said. "Great."

"I heard on the weather report that it only ever got this hot in November once before."

"Wow. I didn't know that."

Now it was weather.

"Cindy," I said.

She looked at me a moment and then reached over and touched my hand. I went through the usual mixture of feelings, resentful, happy, and scared. A lot of fear.

Her hand was touching mine now but she'd take it away eventually. And then she might never touch me again.

My entire body – my entire consciousness – was alive and vibrant with the feel of her flesh.

But soon enough I'd be banished to the darkness again.

"I don't blame you for hating me," she said.

"God, Cindy, I don't hate you, I love you."

"You shouldn't love me, Spence. You should hate me."

"Oh, Cindy."

"There's something you don't know and that I can't tell you and until I figure a way out of it then I can't see you or anybody else."

"Except Myles."

She wore an emerald green sweater and jeans today. Her shining dark hair was pulled back into a playful little ponytail with an emerald green ribbon.

"You don't understand about Myles," she said.

"No, I guess I don't."

"I don't love Myles."

"Really?"

"I don't even want to see Myles."

"Then why do you see him?"

"That's the part I can't tell you."

"Oh."

"Maybe someday I will."

I thought of Josh again. Making a fool of yourself over women and all. And how they like it.

"I'll wait for you, Cindy."

I ached all over. It was like having the love flu. Every ounce of flesh, every piece of bone ached to possess Cindy Marie Brasher.

"That's sweet of you, Spence."

"I mean it."

"I know you mean it. And that's why it's so sweet. But for right now – I don't know what to do, Spence. You can't help me – nobody can."

Then she looked at her watch. "I really have to get back with the girls, Spence."

"I know."

"I just want you to know that I'm sorry for how I've acted the past week or so. I really am. I was a real bitch to you."

"Don't say that about yourself, Cindy."

"It's true, Spence. A real bitch." She looked about to cry suddenly. "Maybe that'll all change someday, Spence. Maybe we can go back to how things were between us."

"God, Cindy, I sure hope so."

And then she was gone.

Again.

Maybe forever.

I just sat there in a kind of stupor.

And now when I looked at the farmers, I didn't feel superior at all.

Oh, no, when you looked at all their smiles and happiness, you knew that these people knew the secrets to a successful life. Their haircuts might be funny, and their clothes might be four or five seasons out of date, and their conversations might sound kind of dorky, but they looked happy and content.

I got up and left, even though I had absolutely no place to go.

Richard Mitchell, KNAX-TV:

"Earlier in the day, there was some hope among the lawyers that their client would be granted a stay of execution. But Justice Stoddard of the Supreme Court has turned down the last minute plea. Now the only person who can save the prisoner is the Governor. And that's unlikely. This is a Governor who was elected on the promise of bringing back capital punishment to this state."

Tape 22-D, October 15. Interview between Risa Wiggins and her client in the Clark County jail.
A: You said it was like being paralysed?
C: Yeah. Right after I looked down the well, I had this kind of seizure. I mean, I was afraid my arms and legs were going to break, I was throwing myself around so hard.
A: What do you think it was?
C: (Angry) What do I think it was? Are you kidding? It was the fucking alien down in the well.

From a Police Report – September 2. 1903

One of the regular drunks from Carney's Tap found her down by the river. He claimed that he was there relieving himself on his way home. He said he screamed when he saw what had been done to her. Several people in the neighbourhood testified that they heard his scream.

This one was even worse than the one who got her head cut off. I know we're not supposed to put personal opinions in these reports but I need to, Chief. There's no other way I can tell you how awful it was.

He's torn all her clothes off and then cut off her breasts and fingers, and then dug out her eyes, same as the first one.

I saw this raccoon crouched under this bush watching me. He had one of her bloody fingers in his mouth.

17

Just about seven hours later, that same Saturday night, the murders happened, and my life would never be the same again.

After the mall, I went home and laid on my bed and read some old Theodore Sturgeon stories. People don't read him a lot these days but they should because he's not only one of the best science fiction writers of all time, he's one of the best writers period. I look on him as the patron saint of fuck-ups. He was sort of a fuck-up himself, from what I've been able to read about him. Takes one to know one.

"You do what I tell you to, Romeo?" Josh said when he came into my room after taking his Saturday night date shower. He had on a starched white button down shirt, jeans, and a pair of cordovan penny loafers without pennies and without socks. He was also wearing about a quart-and-a-half of Brut.

"Pretty much," I said.

I told him about meeting her at the mall.

"Sounds promising."

"It does?" I said.

"Sure. Sounds like he's got some kind of hold on her and she's trying to break away."

"What kind of hold could he have on her?"

"Who knows? She had those mental problems, you know."

'Yeah. But so what?"

"Maybe she did some real crazy shit and he knows about it and says he'll tell everybody about it if she doesn't keep going out with him. I mean, face it, she's a little bit psycho."

I got mad. I couldn't help it. I didn't like to hear her talked about that way.

"She isn't a psycho. She just had a breakdown."

"Only psychos have breakdowns, Romeo." He grinned at me and I couldn't be mad at him any more. "When you get to be a little older, you'll understand stuff like that."

"I will, huh?"

"Yeah." He grinned again. "So what's up for tonight?"

"Probably go out and drive around."

"Alone?"

"Yeah."

"Boy, you really know how to live. Excitement piled on excitement."

"Better than standing around watching a bunch of high schoolers have puking contests."

The grin again. "I guess I couldn't argue with that one."

He gave me a jaunty salute and left.

When I was younger, I used to go uptown on Saturday night just to watch the arrests for drunk and disorderly. Small town like this, that can be a major source of excitement.

I did pretty much the same thing this Saturday night, except I drove around doing it.

I drove past "Harley & Co." which is the biker bar; and "Blood Sweat & Tears," which is where the construction gangs hang out; and then I drove real slow past "Bronco Billy's," which is where the country and western folks congregate.

The problem was, by nine o'clock, I'd driven past them eight, nine times each and I still hadn't seen anybody come catapulting out the door and land on his head on the pavement and then get up and start punching it out with the bouncer who'd kicked him out, to be followed by sirens and gendarmes.

I was on one of my last passes, losing all hope, when I saw the flasher on top of a cop car go on behind me. So did his siren.

He pulled me over.

"You can get the chair for this", Garrett smiled when he walked up to my window.

"I really do something wrong?"

"Light's out on your back plate."

"Oh."

"But I'm not going to give you a ticket."

"I appreciate that."

I noticed that, as always, he had his hand on the butt of his weapon.

"How're things going?" he said.

"Oh, you know."

"She's still seeing fuck-face, isn't she?"

"Myles?"

"Uh-huh."

"For the time being, anyway."

"For the time being," he said. "That sounds like something *she* probably told you."

"Matter of fact it is."

He shook his head. "About ninety-five percent of what women tell you is bullshit. You got to get a lot smarter about pussy, Spence. You really do. For your sake."

Not only had Garrett become a swaggering cop, no longer recognisable as the kid I'd known, now he was an expert on women in general and Cindy in particular. Like Josh.

"We got to get her away from that sonofabitch," he said.

At first, I was kind of touched by what he said. He liked me enough that he wanted to help me get Cindy.

"She deserves a lot better."

And I knew suddenly that he wasn't talking about me.

He was talking about himself.

"A lot better," he said again.

Then he patted my car door with his hand and said, "Well, see you around, Spence."

"Yeah."

"But get that license plate light fixed, all right?"

"Right away."

18

I took the car over to the DX station. Luckily, they had a light for the license plate.

After that, tired of riding around, I stopped in at the video store and picked up the 1978 version of *Invasion of The Body Snatchers*. I think it's almost as good as the original.

I was passing McDonald's, on the way home, when I suddenly got hungry.

I went in and got a fish sandwich and a vanilla shake and some fries. The place was pretty much empty except for a couple of giggling high school girls in the corner.

I sat at the front window and watched the traffic along Hawthorne Street. I figured out once that Hawthorne Street was at least seventy years old. Sometimes I thought of all the different kinds of cars that had driven up and down on this street, from old boxy Model T's to the big-fin jobs of the fifties. Then I thought of all the people who'd come and gone who'd driven up and down Hawthorne. The passing parade, generation after generation. Sometimes, it made me sad to think about the way Mom and Dad would have to die someday. Then the way I'd have to die, and Josh, and Cindy, and everybody else.

If I hadn't been in the Army, I probably wouldn't have figured out the gunshot for what it was.

But it was a gunshot, all right.

Big city people always have this notion that small-town folks are used to guns. But except for hunting trips, gunfire is not something you hear very often in a town like ours.

Then there was another; and another.

Three shots in all.

I glanced back at the high school girls. They were still giggling.

I looked over at the counter. The two boys wiping everything down didn't even glance up.

None of them had any idea that a gun had just been fired. They probably thought it was a car backfiring or something.

I was curious but there wasn't anything I could do about it.

Anyway, I still had a shake and fries I owed some attention to.

I was just tilting the shake back when I saw Fred Wyman running down the sidewalk. He looked as if he was going to run right past me but when he saw me in the window, he ran into the parking lot, and came straight inside.

Fred lived down the block from us. He was about Josh's age.

He was chunky. He wore a Grateful Dead T-shirt. His fleshy face was glazed with sweat. His breath came in gasps.

"You hear what happened?"

"Huh-uh," I said.

"David Myles."

"Myles?"

"He just killed Nancy Tumbler over at the Stop 'n' Shop."

"Killed her? What the hell're you talking about?"

"Killed her, Spence. Shot her three times in the chest. Blood all over the place. He took off runnin'. They're lookin' for him now."

"Why do you think it was Myles?"

"People seen him. Three eyewitnesses. He took the money and killed her right in front of them. I was just goin' down to the video arcade to tell all the kids." He gave me a half-wave and then turned back to the door.

I sat there.

At the moment, I couldn't think of anything else to do.

Sometimes, things don't quite register in your brain, as if your brain just refuses to accept them.

It was that way with what Fred Wyman had told me. I was ready to believe just about anything terrible about David Myles but I sure couldn't see him as a killer. Maybe in a fist fight; maybe accidentally like that. But robbing a convenience store and then killing the sixty-year-old clerk in cold blood? For one thing, Myles came from a wealthy family. He didn't need to rob a convenience store. For another, even if he wanted to kill somebody with a gun, why would he do it with three witnesses?

So I sat there.

I was going to get Cindy back.

That was a lousy thought to have with Nancy Tumbler, a poor, hard-working woman the whole town liked, lying dead on the cold grey tiles of the Stop 'n' Shop.

But that was the thought I had: that whatever hold Myles had had on Cindy was now gone.

And she was going to come back to me. I got up and carried my tray over to the wastebasket, dumped everything and walked out.

On the sidewalk, I looked west down Hawthorne.

Two blocks away, I could see cop cars and an ambulance and a crowd of people. The emergency lights whipped through the November-bare trees.

I wondered where Cindy was, what she was doing. I thought about calling her at home but decided that that wouldn't be a good thing.

I'd called the Brasher house enough today.

If I was going to win back Cindy, and I was sure I was, I'd need to have her folks on my side. Cindy thought a lot of her folks.

I'd parked my car in the far, deserted corner of the lot. I'd read an article that said you could lose three hundred calories a day just by parking at the extreme end of parking lots you were using. I'd put on four pounds since coming home from service.

I peeked in the side window of my junker and saw something weird. The video tape I'd tossed on the back seat had been moved from the corner to the middle of the seat.

Had somebody robbed me? Everything else looked all right.

But then I thought that maybe I'd made a mistake. I didn't have the world's greatest memory. Maybe I'd only thought I'd put the video in the corner.

As I was opening the car door, I heard something behind me, something I recognised vaguely as shoes scuffling across small rocks on concrete.

I turned just in time to see David Myles running at me. He had a gun in his hand.

"Get in," he said.

I got in.

He ran around and climbed in the shotgun seat.

"Go," he said, slamming the door.

"They're looking for you."

"I know they're looking for me, asshole. That's why I want you to get the hell out of here. I tried hiding in the back seat but Garrett pulled in here and started sniffing around. So I hid behind the dumpsters over there."

"You killed her."

"Drive, you asshole," he said. "Drive."

He had the gun pointed right at my chest.

My bowels did cold and nasty things.

My fingers were trembling so hard I couldn't even turn the ignition on at first.

Was he going to kill me, too?

19

I did what he told me.

He said to go out to the country and that's where we went.

He didn't say much, just mostly stated out the window. There was a full moon painting all the fallen cornfields silver, and glazing the tops of the forest trees.

We didn't see any traffic. The only evidence of human life was in the lighted windows of farmhouses. They looked snug, smug, as if they didn't want to know anything at all about a couple of hick kids riding around in the darkness.

"Why'd you shoot her?"

I had to say something. I couldn't think of anything else to say.

"Just drive."

Then: "You think it was my fucking idea? You think I'd fucking do something like that?"

He was crying when he said this.

"You mean you didn't shoot her?"

He didn't look scary now, all the anger was gone from his face, now he just looked scared and sad, football hero sitting there smelling of after-shave and sweat, shaking like a junkie in a bad movie. He had on his letter jacket. It didn't seem to be giving him much solace right now. Being a football hero didn't count for much after you'd murdered somebody in cold blood.

The gun was in his lap.

He wasn't even holding it.

"I need to see her."

"Who?" But I knew who.

"Go back to town."

"Maybe you should turn yourself in."

He glared at me. "Maybe you should keep your fucking mouth shut."

"You sure? About town, I mean?"

"I have to talk to her."

"We get anywhere near town, the cops are going to see us."

"Can't be helped."

He was looking up at the full moon again, talking to himself

He started crying. It was hard for him, as if he didn't quite know how and needed some practice.

I wanted to hate him but I couldn't. Not quite.

"Myles?"

"Yeah?" he said between sobs.

"Let me take you to the police station."

"They won't believe me."

"About what?"

He didn't say anything for a while.

We drove back to town on a gravel road. Gravel dust plumed up behind us like a ghostly tail.

"I did you a favour," he said, looking over at me.

"You did?"

"Yeah. I took her away from you."

"Some favour."

"You don't know about her, man. Believe me, you don't. That's why I said the cops wouldn't believe me. They wouldn't. You know that time they put her away?"

"Yeah."

"They thought she was making all that shit up, what she told them and everything. But she wasn't. It was true." He turned away from me, back to the moon.

Town lights lined the horizon.

He reached down and picked up the gun again.

"I just need five minutes with her."

"Maybe they'd let you see her after you turn yourself in."

He reached over and grabbed my shoulder so violently that he pulled me up from the seat. "Knock off the shit about the cops. You're taking me to her place. You understand?"

He was shouting at me.

Gravel road became asphalt street, timberland became small bungalows, prairie darkness became street lights.

Cindy lived on the far side of town.

With all the cops looking for him, it was going to be a long drive.

"I didn't mean to kill her." I just looked over at him. "I didn't want to."

I looked back to the street.

"It wasn't me — not really."

He was on that again. If it hadn't been him, then who had it been?

I wondered if he was insane. That was possible. People did that sometimes. just went insane.

I'm not sure just when Garrett saw me. Maybe he picked me up a couple blocks sooner than I realised.

He was used to pulling me over and having a little talk and maybe that was what he originally had in mind.

I didn't realise he was behind us until we'd reached the outskirts of the shopping area, where the lights got about ten times brighter.

That's when he must have seen Myles silhouetted in the front seat.

He hit his cherry and he hit his siren.

Myles came up from a kind of stupor, jerked around for a look behind and then said, "Get me down to J Street and then let me out. I'll be better off on foot."

Garrett rammed us then, doing to me what Myles had done to me a few weeks earlier.

The police car hit us with such impact that I was knocked into the kerb.

"Don't stop!" Myles shouted, pushing the gun into my face. He looked lurid, sweat like silver blisters all over his face, dark eyes bulged and crazed, tears running from his eyes.

We went up over the kerb and crashed back down.

"Step on the gas!" Myles shouted.

Then we were doing sixty mph down a narrow town street. I just hoped nobody stepped out in front of us.

Garrett rammed us again.

This time he knocked us up and over the kerb completely.

We skidded across dew-wet grass, through a shrubbery, through a picket fence, and right up to the front door step of some elderly people who were just now peeking out their front window.

When we stopped, I saw that Myles had struck his head against the dashboard. He looked dazed. The gun was on the seat next to him.

I grabbed it, got the door open and crawled out of the car.

Garrett was on the lawn now, gun drawn.

"Get away from the car, Spence," he said, walking closer and closer to Myles' door.

I hobbled away, my knee painful and bleeding from where I'd cut it on the underside of the dash.

Garrett was at the door now.

He approached cautiously and then said, "Come out of there, Myles. Right now."

"He doesn't have a gun anymore, Garrett," I said.

"Just shut up, Spence," he said. "This is police business."

Sirens in the distance, rushing here.

Dark lawn. Two scared oldsters peeking out the window. Garrett in Clint Eastwood stance, gun drawn.

Myles inside the car.

I heard him say: "I want to see her."

"Shut the fuck up and get out of the car."

"You hear me? I said I want to see her. She can explain all this."

"You're never going to see her again, asshole. I can promise you that."

Sirens. Closer.

Garrett raising his Magnum.

Me wanting to shout out that Myles didn't have his gun anymore.

And then Myles saying: "I want to see her, man. That's all I'm asking you. I want to see her."

That's when the two shots exploded in the night. Right through the open window, they went.

Right into Myles' chest.

I'd never heard a man die before. The sound was kind of funny, kind of a cry and kind of a grunt, and then a slumping forward, and then a long deep silence.

The silence scared the shit out of me. Then Garrett walked over to the car and looked inside.

"Oh, Jesus," he said. "Oh, Jesus Christ."

Then there wasn't any silence at all, not for a long time, not with the cop cars and the ambulance and the coroner's van and all the fascinated onlookers and then the weeping family of David Myles.

They took me down to the police station and I was there for six hours and when I got out there were a bunch of reporters there and then Josh had me by the arm and he was pushing me through the crowd and out into the chilly prairie night.

Garrett hadn't merely shot David Myles. He'd executed him.

That was the only thing I could think of all that night as I lay awake still shaking from everything that had happened.

He'd known Myles didn't have a gun. He'd executed him.

Part Two

1

"I'm sure he didn't hear you."

"I said it real loud."

"Spence, put yourself in his position," Chief Stewart said.

Paul Stewart had been the police chief in this town ever since I was in grade school. He was generally considered to be fair, open-minded, and not at all impressed with his badge, the way some cops get.

But he was protective of his cops to the point of obstinacy.

He sat on the edge of his desk and looked down on me in my chair.

"It's dark," he went on. "You've just seen a car crash up through a fence. You approach it with your gun drawn. And then in the front seat, you see somebody who has just murdered somebody else in cold blood. You don't think you'd be a little scared?"

"Sure, I'd be scared but –"

"You don't think you might be totally focused on the killer in the car?"

"Sure, I'd be focused on the guy in the car but –"

"And if somebody said something to you, don't you think there's a possibility that you might not hear them?"

"Sure, there's a possibility but –"

"And that's what happened last night, Spence. He's a young cop and he wanted to be sure he handled the situation the proper way – and he was also scared. It was real easy for him to imagine that Myles had a gun in his hand and was bringing it up to shoot him."

I didn't say anything for a time, just sat in his sunny office with the four filing cabinets and the big desk with framed photos of his grandkids all over it and a wall filled with awards and plaques and a few pictures of the Chief with minor celebrities. The one of him shaking hands with Hulk Hogan struck me as pretty funny.

"That's what happened, Spence."

"He thought that Myles had a gun?"

"Right."

"And when he approached the car, he thought he saw Myles bringing the gun up?"

"Yes."

"And so he shot him?"

"Right."

"Twice?"

"As any good cop would."

"Good cops shoot unarmed citizens?"

He looked at me a long hard time. He was in his crisp dark uniform as usual and his hair was white and his face was old-man fleshy. But the blue eyes were young and smart. And now they were just a little bit mean. He was pure cop.

"You trying to piss me off on this thing, Spence?"

"No, sir."

"Good. Because I like you and I want to keep on liking you."

I stared out the window. Thanksgiving was three days away and the sky was June blue.

"I just wanted to tell you what I was thinking, Chief," I said.

"I appreciate that, Spence."

"I really did yell over to him. You know, that Myles didn't have his gun anymore."

"I believe you, Spence. I also believe that Garrett didn't hear you."

"I guess that kind of wraps things up, doesn't it?"

"Far as I'm concerned, it does." Then: "Spence?"

"Yes?"

"This is a small town. rumours get started pretty fast."

"I won't say anything to anybody."

"I'd appreciate that."

He stood up from his desk and put a beefy hand out, one that mine disappeared inside of.

After we shook, he walked me to the door and clapped me

on the back.

"You miss the Army?"

"Not really."

He smiled. "I was the same way. Couldn't wait to get out of it. That was forty years ago, back when they still had a draft."

He opened the door for me.

"Spence?"

"Yes."

"I know you're not satisfied with our little talk this morning but I'm not trying to hide anything at all. Far as I'm concerned, Garrett was discharging his duties by the book. I would've done the same thing myself in those circumstances. And so would you."

"Maybe I would have."

"And anyway –" He hesitated a moment, as if not sure he wanted to say what he wanted to say. "Save a lot of heartache. In the community, I mean. Putting all of Nancy Tumbler's people through a trial – Hell, it wouldn't have been very easy for Myles' folks, either."

"No, it wouldn't have been."

"And we know he did it."

"Yes, we do."

"There were witnesses."

"Yes, there were."

"So in the scheme of things –"

I guess I couldn't disagree with that part of it. Myles really had killed a woman in cold blood. And a trial would just make the whole town suffer even more.

But there was one thing Chief Stewart wouldn't acknowledge – that his officer had heard me tell him that Myles was unarmed, but had proceeded to execute him anyway.

"You have yourself a good day, Spence."

"You, too, Chief."

This was Monday morning right after breakfast.

When I finished at the police station, I walked over to the department store and went to work.

By noon, just about everybody who worked in the store had come up to me and asked me if I'd been scared after Myles carjacked me. I didn't blame them. They worked hard at drab, empty jobs for very little money and no security. They needed some kind of excitement and management wouldn't let them watch TV during the day so I was the next best thing.

On my lunch hour, I finally worked up the nerve to call Mrs Brasher.

"Well, Cindy's in school," she said, sounding surprised that I'd choose now to call.

"It was you I wanted to talk to, Mrs Brasher."

"Me?" She sounded even more surprised.

"I want to bring Cindy a present – something that'll help take her mind off things – and I was just wondering if you could maybe give me an idea of what she'd like."

Long pause. "I don't think Cindy wants to see you anymore, Spence. So I'm going to ask you not to try and contact her in any way."

The queasiness was back in my stomach. "Why wouldn't she want to see me anymore?"

Another pause. Then a sigh. "She thinks that she helped drive David to – you know, Saturday night – that if she hadn't started seeing you, maybe he wouldn't have gone insane."

Right, I thought. He would have just kept on beating her.

But then I thought of Myles' face in my car a few minutes before he died – the grief, the terror.

"She's going to start seeing Dr Granger again. She's – not doing very well at the moment." Granger was the town's one and only shrink. "She went to school but I wouldn't be surprised if she came home early."

122

"I want to help her, Mrs Brasher."

"Then stay away from her, Spence. I don't mean to be harsh − but that would be best for everybody. And now I have to go."

The rest of the day I kept tearing up and breaking into fits of trembling. I wanted to vomit but when I went back to the john, all I did was peer down into the toilet bowl.

− I'm going to ask you not to try and contact her in any way.

− Stay away from her, Spence.

I really did want to puke.

At first, I didn't recognise him.

This was right near closing time. It had been a slow business day. I'd spent most of my time in the back room rearranging some old stock and marking it down for an upcoming sale. Some of the shoes make you wonder what consumer the manufacturer had in mind. One pair had platform heels, ankle straps and a flowery bow that went across the instep. Apparently, Carmen Miranda was coming back in vogue.

"Are you Spence?"

As I said, I didn't recognise him at first.

He was a small, quiet-looking man with a receding hairline, sad brown eyes, and a forlorn little mouth.

"Yes, I am," I said.

He put out a small hand. "I'm Don Myles, David's father."

"Oh."

I shook his hand. I had no idea what to say. He obviously didn't either. I felt kind of sorry for both of us.

Then the irony of it struck me. It happened this way sometimes, little grey guy like this siring a strapping handsome superstar like David. Recessive genes, maybe.

"I'd like to ask you a favour but I don't want you to feel

obligated about it in any way."

"All right, I said.

"The missus was wondering if you might possibly stop over at our place after the funeral."

"Your place?"

He nodded. "She'd like to talk to you about how David was."

"I see."

"The last hour or so."

"Right."

"If he said anything particular."

– Tell my Mom and Dad how much I love them, Spence. Tell them that I sure wish I would have listened to them.

That's what Mr Myles hoped that David had said.

The poor shambling bastard, standing there so sad, utterly destroyed, the rest of his life never to be the same again,

"I'd be happy to, Mr Myles."

"Really. You wouldn't mind?"

"No; no problem."

I was going to make something up. I'd have to think about it. If I made it too corny, they'd know I was making it up. I'd have to think of something that they'd keep with them the rest of their lives.

"How about if I call you?"

He stared at me and then averted his eyes a moment. "I know what he did to you. Ramming your car that night."

"Don't think about that, Mr Myles. I wasn't hurt bad."

"It was her. He changed after he met her. I'm not saying that he wasn't wild before but – but after he started hanging around with that Cindy Brasher –" He shook his head.

"The missus really would appreciate you stopping by, Spence."

"My pleasure, Mr Myles."

He nodded, and went quietly away.

2

I smelled snow on the wind as I came out of the store that night. Winter always comes abruptly in these parts. Even though the day had been sunny and warm, tomorrow could be white and bitter cold.

Dusk was coming earlier, too. By 5:45, darkness covered everything. The parking lot lights looked dim and ineffective against the vast gloom.

I got in my car and had my first winter encounter with the engine. Damned thing didn't want to start.

I watched as all the other cars pulled out of the lot, owners waving goodbye. A few were nice enough to shout that they had jumper cables but I waved them on. I figured I could do this myself.

Then I was alone and when I looked up at the light, I saw the first few whipping traces of snow.

I tried the engine again and this time it caught but just as it did, I saw a car pull next to mine, and a familiar face looked over at me.

He was out of his car and into mine in moments.

"You need a better car."

"Thanks for the tip," I said.

"I've got a lot of good advice for you, Spence."

"Yeah, I'll bet you do."

"Especially about Saturday night."

I didn't say anything for a time, just sat there and looked out at the whipping snow. "The Chief talked to you, huh?"

"As far as I knew, he had a gun, Spence. That was why I shot him."

"Right."

"Don't fuck with me, Spence. I'm not that shitty little punk you used hang out with. I'm a lot different these days."

I turned and looked at him. "Yeah, I noticed that Saturday when you killed Myles."

125

"He killed Nancy Tumbler."

"That didn't give you the right to execute him."

Now it was his turn to pause. He let out a long, ragged sigh. "I want you to drop this, this whole thing, you understand?"

"You're safe, Garrett. The Chief believes that you didn't hear me say he was unarmed."

"I didn't hear you say it."

"Right."

"I don't give a shit if you believe me."

"I noticed that."

"It's over and done with. There's going to be an inquest and an investigation, and then the Chief said it'll be over."

"Sounds like it's going to be a great investigation."

He opened the door.

The cold air felt good. Clean.

"He used to beat her up."

"Yeah, he did."

"And as I remember, he also beat the hell out of you."

I didn't say anything.

"So what's the big deal? If I didn't kill him, he would have just rotted in prison the rest of his life anyway."

"You're rationalising, Garrett. There wasn't any reason to shoot him and you know it."

Another sigh. "I don't want you talking to the Chief anymore, you hear me?"

"I hear you."

He reached over and put a hand on my shoulder. It was a surprisingly gentle hand. "You're a nice guy, Spence. You really are. I've got a lot of good memories about you, Conan and all that bullshit. So I'm asking you, don't push it anymore, all right? I did what I had to do Saturday night, and it's that simple. If you want to believe that I murdered him, that's up to you. But I'm trying to be a good cop for this town and I don't want that kind of rumour undermining me. So I'm asking you to keep your opinions to yourself." He paused. "I really didn't hear you say he was unarmed, Spence. I really didn't."

I almost liked him right then. He was almost the geeky kid I'd hung out in bookstores with. Conan and all that bullshit, as he'd just said.

And I almost believed him, too. Maybe there'd been wind and he hadn't heard. Or maybe it was as simple as the Chief had said. Maybe when you were approaching a car with a dangerous man inside, your mind was totally fixed on that moment, and you just tuned out everything else.

I guess I wanted to believe that right then, guess I wanted to believe that the world was a safe and sane and trustworthy place after all, and that a cop wouldn't shoot somebody without justification, and then lie on top of it.

Not in this nice old world of ours, he wouldn't.

He took his hand away. "I still think we should go have a pizza sometime and then go have a few brews somewhere."

But then he said, "He didn't deserve her, Spence. She's a very special girl."

And then I knew he was lying.

And knew why he'd killed Myles.

Because of Cindy.

"You going after her now, Garrett?"

The smile was almost a smirk. "You're a little behind the times, Spence. I've already been seeing her."

"What the hell you talking about?"

He got out of the car and started to shut the door. Just before he did, he said, "She asked me to take her to the Christmas dance, Spence."

The smirk was still there.

He closed the door quietly, and walked away.

I let him pull out before I tried the motor again. It was twenty minutes before the engine turned over.

3

Thanksgiving came and went in the usual way. Mom slaved away in the kitchen all morning, we had our feast, then Dad, Josh and I settled in to the living room to watch some serious football.

I had trouble concentrating though. All I could think of was what Garrett had said to me about Cindy asking him to the Christmas dance.

The next day, I became a criminal.

There was a new state law that prohibited one citizen from following another citizen. The anti-stalker law had been voted in after two women, in the same week, had both been killed by stalkers.

I was a stalker.

The first night, I only followed her for an hour. She led me out to the mall. I waited thirty, forty minutes for her to reappear but then got so bored that I just drove on home.

The second night, I got more adventurous. She went to a movie with three girlfriends. Once she was inside the Cineplex, I drove over to a tavern, drank two slow beers and played a little bumper pool, and then eased back out to the movie house just about the time the film was ending.

Cindy and her friends went to get a pizza. I guess I was mostly trying to see if she met up with Garrett any place. She didn't, not in the half hour I sat down the street from the pizza place.

The third night, I knew right away something was going to happen.

She drove straight from her house to a city park that had been closed down for the winter. The temperature was just barely twenty. The snow flurries were starting to get serious.

Following her wasn't easy.

The park was heavily forested and the roads narrow. Even if I hung back as far as a half mile, she'd be able to see me in her rear view.

128

The park looked lonesome, all shorn tree limbs and empty tennis courts and battened-down concession stands.

Where was she going?

She went all the way through the park and then turned down a short gravel road that led to the boat docks.

A few houseboats bobbed darkly on the cold water. A stray dog, hungry and sad, sniffed around the rusty door of one of the boats.

She parked and got out of the car and walked down to the dock.

She looked small and vulnerable against the winter night, bobbing up and down with the turbulent water.

I'd parked my car behind a copse of trees on the hill above and looked down on her now with my binoculars.

The car appeared without warning, headlights garish in the darkness.

As it passed me, going down the steep slope to the docks, I could see that it was a police car.

The car stopped right at the waterline. He cut the beams down to the fog lights.

When he got out, he stretched lazily, not seeming to acknowledge her in any way.

Then he strolled over to the walk and started across the bobbing boards toward her, a kind of lazy insolence in his step. In just a month on the force, Garrett had already become the worst sort of cop.

He took her in his arms and kissed her.

It was that sudden.

He walked up to her, slid his arms around her, brought her to him, and kissed her.

For a long moment, they were one in the night, two darknesses fused.

Then they separated and started walking together toward the far end of the dock, their bodies finding the rhythms of the chopping waters, undulating in a way that was almost comic.

They didn't seem to be looking at each other as they conversed. They just walked and talked. No touching. No more kisses.

When they came to the end of the boards, they stopped and stared out across the water to the bluffs silhouetted on the far side of the river.

This time, she took him in her arms. I could almost feel the smooth touch of her fingers on the back of my head as she pulled me to her for a kiss. I could taste her mouth again, her sex, see the way the moonlight painted her naked breasts in the back seat of the car. It had been like a space capsule, my little car, us all snug and warm inside of it, her loving me as she'd loved no others even if she had given them her body – a space capsule blissfully lost in space, just the two of us, for all eternity.

And now she was bringing Garrett to her as she'd brought me to her.

That queasy mixture of rage and grief worked through my stomach again.

I leaned against the cold black tree and thought how foolish and pathetic I must look – spying on a girl who no longer cared anything about me.

I left.

Got in my car and left.

She could have him, then.

There was nothing I could do about it anyway.

By the time I got home, a bitter wind had swept down from the hills. In my room I pulled out the skin magazine and tried to interest myself in that but I was beyond the lonely solace of masturbation.

I couldn't read, either.

I just lay there with the light out wanting to cry but I couldn't even do that.

She was lost to me, forever.

"Oh, Lord," Mrs Myles said, and started crying.

In high school we studied a playwright named Henrik Ibsen. He believed that there is a good kind of lying and a bad kind of lying. The good kind is when you keep something from someone so as not to hurt his feelings. Or you invent something to tell him so he'll feel better.

Mr Myles had stopped by the store again that day – three days following my last glimpse of Cindy at the boat dock – and asked me if I could stop over at their place tonight.

David Myles had been popular because he'd been a good looking football star, not because his parents had money. They lived in a fading crackerbox in one of the town's first housing developments. The living room was surprisingly cheery, the couch and arm chairs in good condition. The walls were a bright buff blue, complementing the deeper blue of the furnishings. There was a bookcase filled with book club bestsellers. From the kitchen came the pleasant smells of a good dinner.

Mr and Mrs Myles vaguely resembled each other. They were both worn looking, and every word they spoke was filled with apology. He wore a cardigan sweater and a white shirt and slacks. She wore a ruffled white blouse and dark slacks. They looked like two people who'd played parents a long time ago in a fifties sitcom. Strapping David Myles really must have come from their recessive genes.

The moment she started crying, Mr Myles leaned across the couch and put his arm around her.

I wondered if I'd done the right thing.

I'd been here twenty minutes, giving them a highly cleaned-up version of that terrible Saturday night. Good lies, mostly of omission.

But then I decided to tell a few lies for their sake. And so when Mrs Myles asked me, "Did he say anything about us?" I said, "He said he wished he'd been a better son, and that he loved you very much."

But now that I saw her sobbing, I wondered if I'd done the

131

right thing after all.

Mr Myles got her calmed down and she looked over at me and said, "He really said that?"

"Yes, he did."

"That's what people didn't understand about him."

"Ma'am?"

"How sweet he was. Inside, I mean."

"Yes, ma'am."

"They just saw the aggressive football star."

"Yes, ma'am."

"They didn't see the sensitivity and the caring."

"Yes, ma'am."

"He really was a good boy," Mr Myles said. "A lot of people didn't know that."

"It was her," Mrs Myles said, fingering the brooch that she wore on the front of her ruffled white blouse. "That Cindy Brasher."

"I guess I don't know what you mean, ma'am."

"My wife thinks that she got David to believe all *sorts* of crazy things, and that that was why he snapped and – Well, why it all happened." He gave her a tiny hug again, as if to second her theory.

"What sort of crazy things?" I said.

"All sorts of crazy things. You should hear the tapes. Right, George?"

He nodded. "David always had a good, level head on his shoulders but then he started acting really –" He shook his head. "And it started when he met that Brasher girl. Started right away, too."

"We could barely recognise our own son," Mrs Myles said, "the way he was carrying on."

"You mentioned tapes, Mrs Myles."

"On his little tape recorder. He used it instead of a journal."

"I see."

"We didn't find them till the other night," Mr Myles said.

132

"We tried to give them to the Chief of Police but he wasn't interested." For the first time, she sounded not only sad and angry but bitter. "You listen to those tapes and you'll see what we're talking about."

"I'd like to hear them, Mrs Myles."

She glanced up sorrowfully at her husband. She was speaking to me but she didn't take her eyes from him. "Wait till you hear him start talking about the well."

I knew better than to act disturbed or excited. I just said, "I really would like to hear them, Mrs Myles. I feel a kind of – bond, I guess – with David. After Saturday night –"

She nodded solemnly.

"There was no reason for that Garrett to kill him, either," she said. "David didn't have a weapon."

I didn't want to tell her that I'd called out to Garrett. It would only make her feel worse, and there was no solution for it, anyway.

"You ever been out there?" Mr Myles said.

"Out there?"

"To that old cabin in the Hampton woods."

"I guess so," I said, casually as possible. "When I was a kid."

"There's on old well out there," Mr Myles said.

"He became obsessed with it," Mrs Myles said.

"And that's the right word for it, too," Mr Myles said. "Just wait till you hear these tapes. I really believe my son was clinically insane at the time of his death."

"And she did it, that Brasher girl," Mrs Myles said.

"She did it. Putting all the crazy stuff in his head."

We talked for another fifteen minutes, and then Mr Myles went and got two tape cassettes, dropped them into a manila envelope, and handed them over to me.

"You tell me if this doesn't sound like a boy who's clinically insane," he said.

By the time I reached the door, Mrs Myles was sobbing again.

4

I started following Cindy again two days later.

During that time, she met Garrett four different times, twice at the mall, once at a closed skating rink, once in a parking lot behind an abandoned warehouse. At the warehouse, they got into some very heavy sex. In the front seat of his cop car, no less. The way she was straddling him, I was pretty sure they were doing the deed.

All the time I followed her, I had David Myles' cassette tapes playing on the portable player on my front seat.

I could see why his parents had been so disturbed, and why they thought he had gone insane.

He spent most of his time talking about the nightmares he'd had ever since he'd gone to the well with Cindy.

He saw alien creatures, he saw a strange aircraft, he saw an old man, one hundred years ago, lowering an infant into the well.

And he saw himself in a mirror transformed into a creature that made him scream.

Over and over again, he talked about one night at the well, Cindy standing next to him, when he saw a blue glow deep down in the well.

He talked about how the glow was very hot, made him begin sweating in fact, and seemed to coat his skin with an invisible but faintly sticky coat of moisture.

Then he talked about begging Cindy not to make him go back to the well anymore.

That's how he expressed it.

That she was "making him" go. As if she had this power over him.

Toward the end of the second tape, he began to disintegrate completely.

He became so psychotic he couldn't tell the difference between his nightmares and reality.

He mentioned setting fire to a school bus filled with young children and watching it burn.

He mentioned smothering his mother to death in her sleep, and then disembowelling his father with a butcher knife.

He mentioned raping a ten-year-old girl.

He was tormented by the fact that he couldn't tell for sure if these things had happened or not.

I must have listened to the tapes ten times in three days. Some of it I got used to, some of it I didn't.

The crying was the worst of it. I kept thinking of how he'd been in the car right before he died, the sudden weeping. He sounded like that on the tape. It was terror, that's what I was listening to, and it scared me.

Josh stood in my doorway. He said something but I couldn't hear him.

I lay on my bed with the headphones on, listening to David Myles' tape.

I took the headphones off.

"I'm sorry, Josh. What'd you say?"

"I said that must be some great tape, the way you've been listening to it the last couple days. You going to let me hear it?"

I figured he might ask me about the tape I played over and over so I was ready with my answer.

"It's disco."

"Oh, bullshit," he said.

"No, really. Big hits of the '70s."

"Disco sucks."

"Yeah, I read that on a bumper sticker."

"You're really listening to disco?"

"Yeah, I really am."

He shook his head. "Well, I guess I don't need to hear it

then."

I smiled. "Sorry."

He leaned against the doorway. He wasn't just looking at me, he was examining me. "How you doing?"

"Oh, pretty good."

"You haven't been around much lately."

"Yeah. I know."

"The folks're kind of worried about you."

"I'm fine."

"They think you're still pretty depressed about Cindy Brasher."

"I guess I am. At least a little."

"You look real tired."

"I'm fine, Josh. Honest."

"You hear who she's going on with?"

"Uh-huh."

"He's a fucking dork."

"Yeah, he is. But then so am I."

"You're not a dork. You're a dweeb. And there's a difference."

"Oh, yeah, like what?" I laughed.

"Well, a dweeb can change."

"Oh?"

"Yeah. If somebody wants to take the time and energy to show a dweeb how to be cool, a dweeb can make it, eventually. But a dork —"

"Hopeless?"

"Dork is a state of mind. At least the way I see it. No matter how hard a dork tries to change, he can't."

"That's good to know."

"This is serious shit, brother. I hope you're paying attention."

"So what you've been doing, with the fashion tips and everything, is —"

"— trying to undweeb you."

136

"Well, I appreciate it."

"But there's no hope for Garrett and Cindy's out of her mind to go out with him. He thinks he's king shit, the way he struts around all the time. The kids think he's dork number one."

"I'll let him know your feelings."

"I ain't afraid of him, brother. Not even with that big Magnum of his. In fact, all the kids on the team think somebody's going to take that gun of his away from him and put it up his ass."

"Now there's a pleasant image."

He didn't say anything for a moment, then. "I'm on the yearbook committee with Cindy. I'm going to have a little talk with her."

"No," I said, "please don't."

"I just want to find out what's going on. Why she dumped you."

"It'll really piss me off if you bring it up to her."

He shrugged. "Just trying to help."

"I know. And I appreciate it. But just let things lie."

"Then you let Mom and Dad know you're all right."

"I'll do that. I promise."

He nodded to the tape recorder and then did a little imitation disco dance. "You going to start wearing platform shoes and stuff like that?"

"I figured I could borrow a couple pairs of yours."

"The red ones, fine. The pink ones leave alone."

"I'll remember that."

He started to walk away and then stopped. "You sure you don't want me to say anything to Cindy?"

"Positive."

"I could tell her about the difference between dorks and dweebs."

"Then she'd come running to me, huh?"

"She would if you weren't wearing platform shoes."

"Thanks, Josh."

"I just want you to be happy, man."

"I know. And I will be. I'll get over this."

He nodded and left the room.

I put the headphones on and started playing the tape again.

I'd left David Myles in mid-scream.

5

The next night, they went to the well together.

I'd been following her since just after dinner. She went to the library, she went to a friend's house, and then she started to drive home, but suddenly turned west on a street leading out of town.

Fifteen minutes later, she pulled up on the county road running past the woods.

Garrett was already there. He sat in his own car, a two-year old Pontiac Firebird. This must have been his night off.

She parked behind him, on the edge of the gravel, and walked up to his car.

He got out.

Their kiss was immediate, and long and deep. I looked away.

The jealousy was the worst part of all this. It made me frantic. I sensed that someday I wouldn't be able to control myself.

They went up the hill to the woods holding hands.

That made me even more jealous than the kiss. In a strange way, holding hands is more intimate than kissing. It signifies that there's a real relationship there.

I sat up on the hill behind them, pulled off to the side just as they were.

I watched them in my binoculars as they crossed the moonlit upslope leading into the woods.

Hansel and Gretel, I thought.

They were silhouettes, and then they were gone entirely, the woods swallowing them up.

I moved.

I wanted to see everything they did at the well.

The snow of the last few days had blown away. The land was a dirty grey and brown. My feet crunched dead leaves, and almost stumbled over an infant rabbit that looked as if it had been ripped apart by a dog.

The woods scared me.

139

All light died.

The path was narrow and twisting. The image of Hansel and Gretel came back, and then the Grimm stories of my boyhood. I had the momentary sensation of being caught up in a dream. I thought of Myles' tapes, his being unable to distinguish between reality and fantasy.

Deep, deep darkness, and then an unnerving silence. Only the occasional crushed beer can, and the red wrapper of a Trojan, and a crumpled cigarette pack reassured me that this was a real place, and not part of some psychotic dream.

I kept walking, still scared.

To either side of the narrow path, demons and goblins huddled in the shadows, ready to spring. Or so I imagined. My sweat was icy.

Moonlight. Finally.

The valley, and the clearing, where the cabin and the well waited –

They had just reached the cabin when I got to the edge of the clearing and put the binoculars to my eyes.

They kissed again, this time their bodies inexorably entwined.

I saw her hand go to the back of his head.

I thought of how she'd done the same with Myles.

And with me.

I looked away.

Even the phantasmagoria of the dark forest was preferable to watching her kiss him this way.

When I looked back, she was pulling him to the well.

He frowned, reluctant to go.

But she tugged on him like a mother with an obstinate child, and eventually they reached the well.

Once more they kissed, and then she led him the last steps to the well itself.

They spoke for a few moments but the only sound I heard was the lonely prairie wind.

And then he looked down into the well.

Just leaned over the edge and looked down.

And then the blue glow appeared, and painted his face.

Or I thought it did anyway.

Was I imagining things just because I'd played Myles' tapes over and over?

Maybe there hadn't been any glow at all, blue or otherwise.

Just as there hadn't really been any strange muffled voice in my head when I'd been at the well.

And then he screamed.

Covered his face with his hands and screamed.

If there had been a glow, there was none now.

But the scream was undeniably real.

And when he was done screaming, he went into a modified version of the seizure that had overcome Myles, his arms and hands twitching into odd angles, his head snapping back constantly.

She took him in her arms, and there was something touching about the maternalism of it, the graceful and loving way she held and caressed him. I thought of the Pieta I'd seen in a museum a few years ago, Christ dead in the arms of the Blessed Mother.

By now, he was weeping, weeping just as Myles had, and she held him even tighter.

And then, again as she had with Myles, she gradually turned her solace into sex, and they dropped to the ground next to the well, and began making love.

I felt rage, but sorrow, too.

There was nothing more there for me to see. Or nothing more I cared to see, anyway. I walked back to my car.

This time, the forest didn't scare me half as much as my own feelings did.

6

"Mrs Brasher, it's me, Spence."

"Oh, hello, Spence."

"I'd like to speak to Cindy if I could."

A pause. "Well, I'll see if she's up."

"I'd appreciate that."

That's when I heard the whispering behind her. This being Saturday morning, they were probably having a late breakfast. Cindy probably heard my name and started whispering to her mother that she didn't want to talk. Her mother, who had cupped the phone with her hand, started whispering back.

Cindy came on.

"Hello?"

"Hi."

"Hi, Spence." Not exactly warm and enthusiastic.

"I wondered if we could have lunch today."

"Don't you have to work?"

"I traded with somebody."

"Oh."

"I really think we should talk."

Pause. "You know I'm dating your friend Garrett, don't you?"

I laughed. "I'm not sure I'd call him my friend exactly."

"He wouldn't be happy. You know, if we had lunch."

"We could always go over to Dover." Dover was seventeen miles away, a small town that swelled in the summer because of the wealthy people who had homes on the river.

"Well —" she said.

"I want to talk to you about some tapes."

"Tapes?"

I wanted to hook her so she couldn't say no.

"Yeah. Right before he died, Myles recorded a couple of cassette tapes." Now I paused. I wanted to make this as dramatic as possible. "About the well."

142

"Oh?"

"Yeah. He was pretty screwed up about it."

"You have the tapes?"

"Uh-huh."

"How'd you get them?"

She was hooked, all right.

"His folks gave them to me."

"His folks? They know about the well?"

"Yeah."

She didn't say anything for a time, then: "What time do you want to pick me up?"

"Around noon."

"Will you bring the tapes?"

"All right."

"I'd like to borrow them."

"For what?"

"You know, just to listen to them, David had quite an imagination."

"I'll bring them along."

"Around noon, then."

"Right."

On Saturday, the National Guard Armory is a busy place.

Weekend warriors from four different counties come here to play soldier. Having served as an enlisted man, I had a slightly superior attitude to the Guardsmen, just as enlisted men who'd seen combat in 'Nam had a slightly superior attitude toward me for having spent my three years in the wilds of darkest New Jersey.

The Armory was filled with trucks covered in camouflage, with rifles being torn down and put back together, and with a lot of guys standing around drinking coffee and eating doughnuts. The Armory smelled of car oil and gun oil and smoke from a lot of cigarettes.

In the back of the vast, echoing warehouse area was a group of small offices.

I went to third door and knocked.

"Yes?"

I opened the door and pecked in.

Dr Wylie, tall, bald, and slightly stoop-shouldered, sat in a chair at his desk. He wore his camouflage uniform. He'd been working on a set of papers. His pen was still poised above them. The office was small but tidy. On the wall behind his desk were several framed degrees.

"May I help you?" he said.

"My name's Spencer. I was in the Army until about three months ago. Friend of mine, Bill Nelson, said you saw him a few times and I was just wondering –"

"Hell, yes. C'mon in and close the door."

Dr Wylie was a weekend warrior himself. But he'd had a long career as an enlisted man before this. His real job was that of psychologist. He had an office two towns away.

A lot of people just getting out of the service have certain adjustment problems. Bill Nelson, a Navy vet I knew, told me that he and some others always went to see Dr Wylie. He didn't charge you anything, and he was really good at calming you down and helping you think through your problems.

He got up and poured us both a cup of coffee.

When we were all settled in, he said, "So how can I help you?"

"It's kind of embarrassing, actually."

And it was.

– There's this alien in this well, see, Dr Wylie and it's going to come out someday and...

"I guess what I want to know is if people can all have the same delusion at the same time?"

"Could you explain that a little more?"

"Well, say I have a dog and I think he talks to me."

"All right."

"And then I tell my best friend and he doesn't believe me but then he starts watching my dog real close, just on the off chance that I'm telling the truth, and then one day he hears the dog talk."

"I see."

"And then he tells somebody else that my dog can talk, and this guy doesn't believe it, either. But then he starts watching my dog, and listening real hard, and then one day he hears my dog talk, too."

"All right."

"But the dog can't really talk. I just imagined it and so did my friends. Does that ever happen?"

He was sipping coffee and nodding his bald head.

"More often than you think."

"Really?"

"Sure. There's even a psychiatric term for it. Shared Psychotic Disorder."

"I guess I don't know what that means."

"It means that one person has a delusion and tells it to somebody else. This second person is suggestible enough to buy into the delusion, too, so he starts believing in it, and he finds other suggestible people, and he gets them to start believing it, too."

"But they really believe it? I mean, they're not faking?"

"Most of them could pass a polygraph test. They absolutely believe it's the truth. We see that with alien abductions all the time."

"Wow."

"That's not to say that there aren't some real alien abductions. I'm not one of those people who rule out all possibilities. But a lot of the cases I've heard of are part of a Shared Psychotic Disorder. Usually happens to people with very creative minds. They're more open to suggestion."

He put down his coffee cup. "Some of your friends trying to convince you of something you find hard to believe?"

145

"Something like that."

"And they all swear it's true?"

"Yes."

He watched me with shrewd brown eyes. "And you're starting to think that maybe it's true yourself?"

I felt my cheeks get hot. I thought of the night I heard a voice out at the well. An alien voice, yet. Creepy crawlies from planet Zanthar or galaxy Glakmo.

"Yeah." I smiled. "It's sort of like an alien abduction."

"I kind of figured."

"And they kept telling me about this creature and then I started hearing it for myself. Out at the well. What did you call that syndrome?"

"Shared Psychotic Disorder. But you mentioned the well. The one out by where the meteor landed last century?"

"Yeah. You know about it."

He smiled. "They've been telling stories about that well for over a hundred years. Wild stories."

"Shared Psychotic Disorder?"

He nodded.

"That's what it sounds like, huh?"

"Very possibly. If you're hearing alien voices."

There was a knock on the door. "Excuse me. Yes?"

A young guy in a blond crew-cut and a camouflage uniform stuck his head in the door. "We're still having trouble with that all-terrain vehicle, sir. I'm not sure it's going to be ready for this afternoon."

"Give it a good try, will you?"

"Yes, sir."

"We built a lot of today's drill around that machine, Corporal."

"Yes, sir. I'll do my best, sir."

He saluted and was gone.

When Dr Wylie looked back at me, I was smiling. I felt great relief.

No aliens in the well.

No voices in my head.

A deeply disturbed young woman named Cindy Brasher had simply imagined the alien properties of the well.

As had Myles and Garrett, when they went into their seizures, the idea for which Cindy had probably planted in their minds in advance.

Just as I'd imagined the voices and the icy blue glow I'd glimpsed the other night.

"God, I'm glad I talked to you." Then, "Does it sound like I'm nuts?"

He laughed. "Not at all. Sounds like you got caught up in what I call the 'campfire syndrome.'"

"What's that?"

"Well, you take a group of perfectly sane adults of average or above intelligence, and you put them out in the woods around a campfire late at night. And then somebody starts telling monster stories, the way kids always did at summer camp. And if you tell the stories long enough and well enough, these perfectly sane and intelligent adults begin to wonder if there isn't something in the woods, after all. So for the rest of the night they're very jittery. Probably can't sleep. And they begin to hear things and see things. That's the 'campfire syndrome.' It's kind of a lower order of the Shared Psychotic Disorder."

"Man, I feel better."

He smiled. "I wish I had this effect on everybody I saw."

"I really appreciate it."

"My pleasure."

I stood up and put my hand out to shake.

He had a quick, hard grip like a snakebite.

"Everything else going all right?"

I felt exultant. No aliens.

"Everything else," I reported gleefully, "is going just fine."

Now I really could help Cindy, and win her back in the process.

7

"Is that my brother whistling?" Josh said, coming into my room as I splashed on some English Leather.

"It certainly is."

"You must've had one hell of a good time last night."

"This morning."

"You already had a good time this morning?" I smiled at him in the mirror.

"Yeah."

"And you're not going to tell me about it?"

"Huh-uh."

He came up and patted me on the back. "I'm just happy to see you happy again."

"Everything's going to work out."

"With Cindy?"

"Everything's going to work out with everything."

"Wow," he said. "The power of positive thinking."

I left earlier than I needed to for my lunch date with Cindy. Drove around. Rock and roll up real loud. My junker felt like a brand-new Corvette.

Shared Psychotic Disorder.

I'd explain it to Cindy. She probably wouldn't agree with it. Not at first.

But eventually I'd be able to convince her. And win her back. I was sure of it.

I was three blocks from her house when I heard the siren.

I looked in the rear-view and saw the police car, red roof lights flashing, signalling for me to pull over.

I pulled over.

No surprise that Garrett was the cop.

No surprise that he swaggered up to my car.

No surprise that he rested his hand, gunfighter style, on the handle of his Magnum.

He walked in a slightly pinched way and when I looked down I saw he wore a brand-new pair of cowhide Western boots.

"You were speeding," he said.

And the truth was, I probably had been speeding.

"I thought you worked nights," I said.

"Got an officer out sick."

"You giving me a ticket?"

"Not if you give me the tapes."

He peered into the car, saw the two cassettes on the seat next to me.

"Cindy called me," he said.

"I see."

"Your date's cancelled."

"You speak for her now, do you?"

"Yeah, I do." He nodded to the tapes. "And I'd appreciate it if you'd hand those over."

"Not a chance."

"I'm trying to be nice about this, Spence."

"Nice. Right."

"I'd just like to hear them. Then I'll bring them back."

I smiled at him. "You ever hear of Shared Psychotic Disorder?"

"Not lately."

"The well and the alien down there – it's all imaginary. You believed her and I believed her and Myles believed her – Myles believed her so much that he went crazy and went out and killed somebody."

"If that's the case, then why should you mind lending me the tapes?"

"The principle of the thing. They don't belong to you."

"You were going to loan them to Cindy."

149

"No, I wasn't. I was going to play them for Cindy."

He was smooth and he was fast, and the way he leaned in to my car, probably no passing motorist could see what he was doing here on this busy street.

The barrel of his Magnum pressed against the side of my head.

"Maybe I'm crazy, too, Spence, just like you say Myles was. Maybe I'll blow your fucking head off right here."

"No, you won't."

"You sure of that?"

But when I glanced up at his eyes, I really wasn't sure. He looked sort of the way Myles had that Saturday night. A little insane but in a hard, cold, controlled way.

"The tapes," he said.

I gave him the tapes.

I was also going to give him a speech and then give him some threats but suddenly I was too weary of it all.

When he'd stuffed the tapes in his trouser pocket, he took the gun from my head, slammed it back in his holster.

"One thing," he said.

I just watched him.

"No more contact with Cindy."

"It's a free country."

"Not where Cindy's concerned." He was so angry, he was trembling now. "Not where Cindy's concerned."

And then he stalked back to his car.

At least he hadn't given me a speeding ticket.

8

I got sick.

For three days I stayed in bed, my mom calling work and telling them that I couldn't come in, the way she used to call school for me.

She'd take my temperature in the morning and afternoon but couldn't find a fever, even though I felt hot and sweaty.

She'd give me cough syrup because I said my chest felt so tight. But I never coughed, and I didn't have any sinus drainage in the back of my throat.

Mostly, I slept.

I didn't eat much, didn't watch TV, didn't even read.

The third day, she came in and opened my curtains and said, "I thought you might want to look at the snow."

It was beautiful, that snow, the kind that you always see on Christmas cards mantling snug rooftops and providing traction for sleighs and snowballs for snowball fights. Sometimes when I saw Christmas card paintings of the turn of the century, I wanted to climb into the picture, and go back there. Life seemed so much easier, then.

"Honey," she said, turning from the window, "I wonder if I could talk to you."

"Sure."

"I mean, without you getting mad or hurting your feelings."

I guess I pretty much expected what she was going to say.

She sat herself on the edge of my bed and said, "It's Cindy, isn't it?"

"What's Cindy got to do with it?"

"Why you're in bed."

"I'm sick, Mom."

"I know you're sick, honey. But it's not the flu or a cough or a cold. It's Cindy."

I dropped my head and started staring at my hands folded on my lap.

"Right before I met your father, I broke up with this young man because I found out he'd been unfaithful. And I got sick, too. I stayed in bed for almost two weeks."

It's always a strange feeling when your parents force you to confront the fact that they were your age once, and went through all the same things you're going through.

The thing is, you secretly suspect that it was easier for them to survive all the perils of youth. Your parents always strike you as a little naive, and you think that naive people can't get hurt as much as hip, sophisticated people like yourself.

"Two weeks?" I said.

"Two weeks. My mother had the doctor come over – they still made house calls in those days – and he examined me and then he asked my mother if she'd step out of the room and then he said, 'I heard about you and Ted Malley.' And all I could say was, 'Oh,' and he said, 'That's why you're sick in bed.' I didn't believe him at first but he explained to me that any time you have a big shock in your life, you can get sick. You don't run a fever or have a scratchy throat or have a headache, but you're still sick. And you really are sick. The doctor asked me if I'd ever heard the expression 'heartsick,' and I said, 'Sure,' and he said, 'Well, that's what this is. You're heartsick. And it's just as real as having the flu or the measles or anything else, But the trouble is, there isn't any medication I can give you. You have to provide your own cure.' I didn't know what he meant. 'You have to get up out of that bed,' he said, 'and force yourself to go on with your life. At first, it'll be very, very difficult, and you'll want to go back to bed and start sleeping all the time again. But if you go on with your life, a little bit at a time it'll get easier for you. And then one day, maybe six months, maybe a year from now, you'll look back and wonder why you ever let yourself get so wrought up about it.' And I asked him how he knew all this and he laughed and said, 'Because I went through it myself. I fell in love with the prettiest girl in the Valley right after I got out of med school, and after we were engaged for about a year, she told me that she still loved the boy she'd been seeing before me. She went back to him then. I had to have another doctor substitute for me for about a week and a half. I took to bed and couldn't get out, All I wanted to do was escape everything by sleeping as long as I could.' So, see, it even happens to doctors."

I think I loved my mom more than I ever have right at that moment, loved her for her kindness and optimism and concern for me.

I threw one leg out of bed and said, "You call work for me this morning?"

"Not yet."

"Good."

"You getting up?"

"Uh-huh."

I leaned over and gave her a kiss on the cheek. "I'm going to take a shower and I'll be down in a few minutes."

"I'll have waffles and bacon waiting for you."

"Thanks, Mom. I really liked that story you told me." I grinned. "By the way, was it actually true?"

She grinned back. "Most of it."

Then she went downstairs, and I went to the bathroom. I hadn't shaved in the three days I'd been in bed, and I had only showered once.

Two nights later, at the dinner table, just as we were finishing our spaghetti complete with the I'M ITALIANO bibs Dad made us wear whenever we ate Italian, Josh said, "We're leaving right at 7:30."

At first, I thought he was talking to Mom and Dad, some event I didn't know about.

"You hear me?"

I looked up from my spaghetti. "Me?"

"You."

"What's 7:30?"

"When we leave."

"Leave for where?"

"For our dates."

"I don't have a date."

Josh winked at Mom. "You do now."

"What're you talking about?"

Dad said, "One of Josh's lady friends has an older sister."

"You should see her," Josh said.

"Wasn't that nice of him?" Mom said.

"So wear your white button-down shirt," Josh said, "and your grey winter jacket and your grey slacks and your cordovan loafers. And go easy on the English Leather. You overdo it sometimes."

"I don't even know this girl."

"It's called a blind date," Josh said.

"But I'm not blind."

This time, he winked at Dad. "For your sake, I hope she is."

She wasn't blind.

She was, in fact, beautifully endowed with all her senses.

Josh went up to the door and got them and when he brought them back and the headliner light went on and she got her first look at me, I could see her disappointment.

She didn't go "ish" or "ick" or run screaming from the beast, but her eyes definitely said that I was not in her league, and she was going to have a not-good time tonight.

Right after the movie, and just about the time Josh was suggesting that we all go out for something to eat, my date said, "I really have a terrible headache. I'm sorry. Gosh, I was having so much fun. I really hate to go home so early but this headache —"

And then she made all the faces one makes when one doesn't actually have a headache but wishes to make others believe that one *does* have a headache.

She was so dramatic about it all that I almost said why didn't we take her to the hospital instead of her house but, I figured why make her think even less of me than she already did?

After Josh dropped her off, he dropped me off at home. His girlfriend kept making apologies for her sister – the headache routine had embarrassed her, I think – and I kept saying it was all right. If only her sister had been half as sweet as she was.

Since it was barely ten o'clock, Mom and Dad were still up watching TV.

I could tell by the look they exchanged that they knew my evening hadn't gone so well.

"Was she a nice girl?" Mom said.

"Pretty much."

"You're home pretty early," Dad said.

"Headache."

"You want some aspirin, dear?" Mom said.

"No. She had a headache."

Mom recognised the implication immediately.

Headache is a code word world-wide for women. Not only does it mean an easy means of escape from having sex, it also provides a way out of myriad other chores.

Such as enduring a night with a dork who is far beneath your station.

"There's some chocolate pie left in the refrigerator," Mom said.

"I guess I'll just go upstairs and listen to some music or something."

Another look between them.

Was I going to take to bed again, go back to my mourning?

"Sure you don't want some pie?" Mom said.

"Letterman's on in another twenty minutes."

"Nah. I think I'll go upstairs."

I must have been feeling at least a little better that night because I slipped my hand beneath my mattress and extracted the skin magazine and then I made sure that my door was firmly closed and then I pleasured myself.

And then an odd thing happened.

Instead of calming me down, and helping me get ready for bed the way it usually did, pleasuring myself made me restless.

I wanted to get up and *do* something.

I had no idea what that might be.

When I went back down, I wore a blue crew neck sweater, jeans, my imitation leather bombardier jacket, and running shoes.

Mom and Dad looked surprised to see me.

"I'm going out," I said.

"Out?" Mom said.

"Out where?" Dad said.

"Riding around, I guess."

"At this hour?" Dad said.

"You said yourself it was early."

Another parental glance was exchanged.

"Are you feeling all right, dear?"

"Fine, Mom."

"You know, if you want to drink a few beers, you're welcome to do it right here. You were in the Army and everything, son."

"Thanks, Dad. I'm just restless is all. I thought maybe riding around would help me." I smiled. "At least I don't want to stay in bed anymore."

Mom nodded, seeing my logic. "That's true, Robert. It is nice to see him up and around."

"You just be careful."

"I will, Dad."

"Very careful, Mom said.

"Very, *very* careful," I said, and left.

After about twenty minutes, you sort of exhaust all the riding-around possibilities of our little town.

I drove past Pizza Hut, Arby's, Motel 6, Holiday Inn, Ramada Inn, McDonald's, Burger King, Long John Silver's.

I drove past the old school, the new school, city hall, the library, I went out by the old skating rink, the new skating rink, the football field and the city park.

It was a cold but lovely winter night, everything a crisp pure white, a full proud moon riding the sky.

I kept driving, punching station to station to find some really heavy duty rock songs. I wanted heavy metal tonight. I needed to feel invigorated.

And then I saw them.

Cindy and Garrett.

In his car.

Her sitting close-as-she-could-get as he drove.

And it happened again.

I wasn't even aware of doing it at first.

I just started following them.

9

The country road was a roller coaster of steep upslopes and equally steep downslopes. There was just enough snow and ice on them to make them dangerous.

I followed Garrett's Firebird deep into the country, the farmhouses getting fewer and fewer the longer we drove, timber becoming more and more dominant.

The moon was behind clouds and the snowy land had a dirty, gritty feeling.

I had no idea where he was going and I wondered if Garrett did. Maybe they were just driving around. Maybe they were having an argument and needed to talk it out and weren't paying any attention to where they were at all.

Then Garrett did a peculiar thing.

About half a mile from the Swenson farm, he cut his lights. He didn't pull over to the side of the road. He didn't even slow down.

He just cut his lights and headed straight for the Swenson place, turning into the gravel drive as soon as he reached it.

He stopped right at the head of the drive.

And sat there.

A quarter mile behind them, I pulled off to the side of the road.

I grabbed my binoculars and got out.

Icy snow crunched beneath my feet. The below zero temperature bit at my nose and cheeks. The night seemed vast and somehow alien, as if I'd been set down on a world that was not quite earth. Only the lonely bay of a timber wolf reassured me that I was still earthbound.

I focused the binoculars and had a look.

They sat in the front seat of Garrett's Firebird, talking.

Garrett smoked a cigarette.

They didn't seem to be arguing – no angry faces, no sudden sharp gestures – but the conversation didn't seem relaxed, either.

Then I saw that Garrett had spread a piece of paper on the dashboard.

He pointed to it, spoke.

Cindy seemed to be listening intently.

He pointed to the paper again, several times.

Then they were up and out of the car.

Mae Swenson was an aged and wealthy widow who kept her farm running with a succession of managers and hired hands. She was no easier to work for than her husband had been, and he'd been known to fire a dozen people in a single month. The Swensons had inherited several large farms from Mae's father. They sold them off back at the peak of land values in the late seventies, when corporations were paying ever-sillier prices for rich black Midwestern soil.

Now Mae had just this one farm.

But according to local legend, Mae had something else, too.

Her own father having lost most of his money in a bank failure, Mae had an almost psychotic fear of banks.

It was said, therefore, that she kept her valuables, including large amounts of money, right in the house with her.

She didn't have any security alarm to protect her, it was further said, nor any kind of security surveillance team driving by.

But she did have Poker.

Poker was a German shepherd that delighted in landing on and tearing to pieces any living thing you put in front of him.

It was said that a little girl came with her folks to visit Mae one sunny Sunday afternoon.

The little girl brought her kitten with her.

Once they were outside the car, the kitten jumped out of the little girl's hand.

Poker took it from there.

Not even Mae herself, who shouted and beat at the German shepherd with a broom handle, could quell Poker's appetite until the kitten was nothing but a bloody carcass.

Poker, it was further claimed, preferred human meat to all else.

A drifter had heard tell of Mae's goodies tucked away inside her house. He decided that he was man enough to overpower a widow woman and take her treasure.

The drifter jimmied one of the downstairs windows and climbed inside.

Poker found him pretty quickly. He'd broken a leg the day before and Mae had kept him inside for a time. Usually he stayed on the front porch.

My dad happened to be downtown that same night, when the ambulance brought the drifter in.

My dad swears that Poker ripped the man's windpipe right out of his throat, leaving only a bloody cavity.

No charges were pressed.

Everybody knew that Poker was a killer and that uninvited guests visited Mae at their peril.

So here were Cindy and Garrett walking up to Mae's house late at night.

I trotted down the road after them. I wanted to get a better look at what Garrett held in his left hand.

My first impression was that it was a pistol. But there was something odd about it – pistol-like but not a pistol. It was the difference between a .38 and a starter's gun for a race. They resemble each other until you look closely.

They went right up to the porch of the large two storey white house with gables and a few spires added to show some creativity.

You could see they were waiting for Poker.

They looked left, right, straight ahead.

Now that they were within his domain, they moved more slowly, carefully.

I could hear them wondering, Where is Poker?

And that's when Poker appeared.

He came straight for them, flying off the porch, his knife-like teeth dripping saliva, his eyes glowing.

I have to say that Garrett was a lot cooler than I would have been in his situation.

He stood his ground.

When Poker was airborne, and about to knock him to the ground, Garrett took two careful steps to the left, raised the weapon in his hand and fired.

If there was a sound, I didn't hear it.

I just saw Garrett's hand jump from the recoil. Otherwise I wouldn't have known he'd fired at all.

Poker's trajectory took the dog a foot past Garrett.

Poker ended up slamming into a snowbank.

The enraged way he pulled his snout from the snowbank, the furious way he turned his long, lean body around to face Garrett, I assumed that Garrett was in deep trouble.

Then Poker collapsed.

No other way to say it.

One moment he was standing there growling, ready to pitch himself at the hated Garrett, and then he was flat on the ground, his head lolling to the left.

Unmoving.

I wondered if he was dead.

Cindy had covered her face, didn't want to see.

Garrett approached the animal, knelt down next to him. He felt for vital signs.

He looked up and said something to Cindy. The way she took her hands from her face, I could tell that Garrett had reassured her that the dog wasn't dead.

Garrett stood up. Walked over to Cindy. Took her in his arms. Kissed her.

I brought my binoculars down.

I still couldn't watch her kissing anybody else.

Then they were moving again, this time toward the house,

walking on tiptoe as they ascended the three steps leading to the porch.

Only on the porch did Garrett show any hesitation. He glanced around, as if looking for something important.

Then he walked over to the door, took a bulky ring of keys from his pocket, and started searching for the proper one.

Cops have as many keys and tools as burglars. That's why a number of cops go bad. Simply can't resist the temptation. Who would suspect a cop of being a B&E man?

Garrett found what he wanted on the tenth or eleventh try.

The front door opened.

The interior of the house, as seen from the front door, was much darker than the night outside.

Then he nodded for Cindy to follow him.

She seemed just a bit reluctant but then walked past him, into the interior.

No lights ever showed.

No sounds were ever heard.

For the next half hour, the house sat as dark and quiet as it had been previously.

There was just the prairie and the snow and the silence, not even any wind now.

The few times I put my glasses on Poker, he was as unmoving as ever.

They came out of the house quickly. Garrett carried a bulging paper sack. Cindy's face was what held me.

Something was smeared all over it.

All I could think of was the war paint Indians used to wear for battles.

Why would she have something smeared all over her face?

I took a closer look at Garrett and saw that his face, too, was smeared with something dark and streaky.

What was it?

When they reached Poker, Garrett laughed.

His foot lashed out and caught Poker in the belly.

The dog didn't move.

Garrett laughed again.

They started walking to the car.

Cindy looked scared.

She said something to Garrett.

He walked over to her, lowered the bag so she could see inside.

And then he laughed again.

Cindy smiled but she still looked scared.

When they reached the car, Cindy got inside right away. Garrett walked to the road and looked up and down.

He didn't want anybody to see him pulling out.

Apparently satisfied that nobody was around, he walked back to the car, opened the trunk, and set the grocery sack inside.

Then he walked to the driver's door, and got in.

He kissed her immediately, and before long I had to look away again.

This time it was worse.

Garrett had slid over on the passenger side of the front seat so Cindy could mount him.

There on the lonely prairie, the car rocked, springs labouring, and Cindy's tiny screams of passion rang in my cars.

At least it was over with quickly.

Garrett backed out with no lights, pointed the car west — away from my car — and took off fast.

Still no lights.

I stood there for a long time listening to the silence. I just kept thinking about those smears and streaks on their faces.

There was only one way I could know for sure if my worst suspicions were right. I'd have to go inside Mae Swenson's house myself.

10

Just inside the front door, I paused. In the Army I'd been around a number of serious accidents, and as a result there was a harsh, iron smell I'd come to know. Blood.

That smell filled this house.

I took a deep breath and walked deeper inside.

There were a lot of antiques in the living room and parlour – pewter mugs and Victorian gas-style lamps and a Charleston Battery Bench among them. There was also a 36-inch TV screen and a very modern couch. Apparently the widow Swenson wasn't long on consistency.

I saw all this in the faint silver moonlight that touched the frosty window panes. The darkening clouds had passed.

I walked over to a staircase and put my hand on the banister and looked upward to the darkness on the second floor.

My hand felt sticky.

I took it from the banister and held it up to the moonlight. I felt the texture, held my hand to my nose. The smell. *That* smell.

I started walking up the steps. I wanted to run back and call the police but I was afraid of getting Cindy in trouble.

I always think of *Psycho* whenever I'm ascending a staircase like this. You know, the scene where private investigator Martin Balsam is going up the stairs to look for Norman's mother. And suddenly there she is, butcher knife and all.

But Norman's mother wasn't here tonight.

I climbed all the way to the second floor without anybody running out of any of the bedrooms.

The second floor was so deep in gloom, I could see only a few feet ahead of me.

The smell was awful up here.

Blood was now mixed with faeces. That's another helpful thing I learned in the Army, how at the last your bowels frequently betray you.

The first door I came to, I pushed inward, and then held my breath, afraid of what I was about to see.

Moonlight revealed a kind of informal den. There was a wall of bookcases and a small fireplace and a twenty-one-inch portable TV on wheels. There was also a desk and a daybed. Neither was an antique but both looked pretty old.

But the most interesting part of the room was the wall safe. It stood open, a virgin violated.

I walked across two shaggy throwrugs and stood in front of the safe.

I peered inside.

I couldn't see anything. Too dark.

I walked over to the desk and started going through the drawers. I'd remembered to pull my gloves on before entering the house. No fingerprints.

In the bottom left drawer, I found a two-battery flashlight. The batteries were dying. The light cast was yellow and muzzy but it was better than nothing.

I went back to the open safe and shone the light inside.

All I found were stocks and bonds, ITT and IBM and other blue chips. There was no money of any kind.

I could make a pretty good guess of where it had all gone.

I walked back down the hall. The flashlight beam was now flickering on and off.

The next door stood ajar.

The stench was overpowering.

I used the toe of my boot to open the door further.

She was completely naked. She lay atop white, blood-soaked sheets. Her hands and breasts had been hacked away. And her eyes cut out.

Her white hair made the scene not only terrible but pathetic. Nobody should treat an old person like that. The blood was even spattered over her white hair. Like decoration.

I walked very close to the bed and then slipped in a pool of blood. I was thrown forward so that my face ended up only inches from her empty gaze of blood. I heard myself scream and quickly pulled myself erect.

Blood splotched and gooped and glopped the wall behind her brass double bed. My sputtering flashlight also revealed pieces of human meat that had adhered to the wallpaper.

I found the bathroom, two doors down, just in time.

After I was finished, tears stung my eyes, vomit burned my throat.

I went back into Mae Swenson's room and took a final look.

She couldn't have done this, I thought.

Or so I hoped. Not Cindy.

Maybe all she did was watch.

I tried not to think of some of the things David Myles had said on his cassettes – things about Cindy.

I turned around, to get out of the room fast, and as I did, I stepped on something.

I didn't want to shine my sputtering flashlight to the floor but some grim impulse made me.

One of Mae's hands.

The simple gold wedding ring looked sad sitting on the hand that had been ripped away from its arm.

Downstairs, the front door slammed shut.

I immediately pictured police.

I'd be up here, trapped, and they'd never believe my explanation.

I ran out of the room and down the stairs.

The living room and parlour seemed much darker than before.

I shone the flickering light around both rooms.

No cops.

The wind had blown the door shut.

I felt drained, then, totally exhausted.

But I had to move and move quickly now.

I forced myself out of the death house, and into the night.

11

I have no idea where I drove for the next hour and a half.

Sometimes I was in town, sometimes I was on county roads.

A couple of times, I even drove by the police station.

– I want to report a murder. I can even tell you who the murderer is.

– Oh, you can, can you?

– Yes, sir, its one of your own officers. Garrett.

– One of our own officers, eh? Well, now, isn't that interesting You're accusing one of my own men of murder?

That's how the cops would react about Garrett.

They wouldn't believe me, they wouldn't want to believe me.

But Garrett wasn't my concern. Cindy was.

Even if she'd done nothing more than watch, she would also be charged with murder.

There was no way I could go to the police.

I stopped at an all-night gas station, its white tiles and bright lights making it look like a huge alien space craft that had just landed in the middle of the rolling dark prairie.

I went in the john and tried to puke.

I couldn't.

I went back to my car and drove away.

And then I made a U-turn on the empty highway and drove right back.

This time, I didn't have any trouble puking at all.

I ate.

That was the funny thing.

After all the terror, and all the puking, I was suddenly,

almost giddily hungry.

I pulled into a truck stop and sat at a counter with several grizzled drivers popping Benzedrine and eyeing the two hookers who were working this particular stop tonight. These were hookers who specialised in truck stops and truck drivers.

They were both pudgy, both barely out of their teen years, and both badly bleached blondes. One of them had a right eye that strayed and almost no breasts at all. I couldn't help it, I felt sorry for her. Being a hooker was a tough life, made even worse with a queer eye and a flat chest.

I ate six pancakes, two orders of hash browns, and a cheese omelette.

I also managed to listen to around twenty-five country and western songs, which is no easy task, let me tell you.

I decided to top off my meal with a slice of apple pie and a fourth cup of coffee.

That was a mistake.

Two bites into the pie, I clamped my hand over my mouth and raced to the bathroom.

A couple of hairy truck drivers standing at the urinal watched me dive for a stall.

When I came out, and went to the sink to wash my face and hands, they were still at the urinal, passing a joint back and forth.

"You better learn to hold your liquor a little better," one of them said solemnly. "You ain't gonna get no pussy with puke all over your shirt."

"Thanks for the advice," I said.

When I got home, around two, Josh sat at the kitchen table nursing a Pepsi and eating a doughnut. The kitchen smelled of coffee and spices.

"How you doing?"

"Pretty good," I said. "Aired, I guess. I went to the late show out at the Cineplex and then I just drove around."

"What'd you see?'

"Oh, that new Kevin Costner movie."

"Any good?"

I shrugged. "Nothing special."

I yawned, exhausted.

"Well, I'm going to head up to bed."

"I'll be up in a little bit," Josh said.

Then I made my mistake.

I stood up from the table and took my jacket off. I didn't think anything of it until I saw Josh's face harden, and a kind of panic come into his eyes. You didn't see Josh panic very often.

"Wow. Are you all right?"

I wore a yellow long-sleeved button-down shirt.

Blood was splotched and splattered not only all over the chest and stomach of the shirt, but also on the sleeves.

I remembered slipping in blood, and falling into the dead woman.

I had picked up a lot of blood.

"I'm fine," I said.

"Where the hell'd you get all that blood?"

"There was an accident on the highway. I stopped to help somebody."

He knew I was lying.

But what else could I do?

"She bled a lot but she didn't get hurt too bad. The woman in the accident, I mean."

He just kept staring at the blood on my chest and arms.

"I'll see you in the morning," I said.

"Yeah," he said, and then he looked at me long and hard and said, "You want to talk about it, brother?"

"There's nothing to talk about, Josh. There was an accident on the highway and this woman was hurt and bleeding and

I helped her and I got some of her blood on me. No big deal."

"Right," he said. "No big deal."

I went up to bed.

Richard Mitchell, KNAX-TV:

"The prisoner has been under a suicide watch for the last month. Round the clock surveillance, including video cameras in his cell. Some of our viewers may remember that a few years ago, a prisoner in Nebraska tried to hang himself in his cell the day before the execution. He was almost dead but the warden insisted that doctors revive him. The next day, the prisoner was executed as scheduled."

Tape 34-D, October 31. Interview between Attorney
Risa Wiggins and her client in the Clark County Jail
A: You say the alien made you do it. I guess you'll
have to explain that to me.
C: The chant.
A: The chant?
C: In my head. Over and over. Telling me what to do.
I tried everything I could to get rid of it but nothing
worked. Finally, I realised the only thing I could do
was do what the alien told me – and then the chanting
would stop.

From a Police Report – September 24, 1903

The thing was, he didn't put up any resistance at all. I found him in a deserted barn on the edge of town. Somebody had come running to the station house to tell me that something terrible was going on there,

His name is Abner. He works as a clerk over at First Bank. Very mild-mannered.

When I got there, I found him sitting there in the middle of the barn. He had a lantern nearby and a completely naked dead woman stretched across his lap. This one, it was her face he mostly mutilated. The eyes were dug out, of course.

He was skinning her.

I drew my service revolver and walked over to him and told him to put down the mule knife he was using to skin her.

He put the knife down, the naked woman with most of her skin stripped off still on his lap, and he said, "I didn't want to kill any of them, officer. I really didn't."

Then he started telling me about this well up by one of the line shacks the electric company uses. He said there was some kind of Martian or something in the well and that it was the Martian who was making him kill all these women.

All I could think of was when that meteor crashed out there several years back. Bunch of town kids started the story that there were Martians inside the meteor – like it's some story by HG Wells, they said – and that the Martians were going to take over the entire planet.

There was a lot of fuss when that rumour started, and even some adults, who should've known better, started to believe it.

This Abner Fenton was apparently one of the adults who believed it.

When I told him it was time to put the handcuffs on him, he just nodded to the dead woman's right arm and said, "I'm almost finished with her arm. Couldn't I just have a few more minutes?"

I picked up the knife and put my gun on him and told him to set the woman on the floor and stand up.

He never gave me any more trouble the rest of the night.

12

By morning, Mrs Swenson's body had been discovered, and I quickly got the feeling that our little town was never going to be the same again.

In big cities, even the most heinous of murders are quickly forgotten, unless one of the killers or victims is famous.

But a small town is like a family, and when one of your own is murdered, the death becomes very personal.

Especially given the way that Mae Swenson was butchered.

Downtown talk was of nothing else. The women looked scared, the men looked angry.

A small group of hunters over at Al's Diner talked about getting a posse together and hunting down the killer in the woods, where they were sure he was hiding.

They just couldn't believe that anybody from our town could murder somebody this way.

All kinds of rumours and theories were floated.

Because we live within fifty miles of a prison, there was talk that a multiple-murderer had escaped and killed Mrs Swenson. According to this story, the killer was black. Of course.

Another rumour had it that a biker gang did it. The town had always hated this gang, and pretty much forced it to keep to a single tavern down by the railroad spur. I guess the Chief actually did ride out to the old quonset huts where the bikers lived – and mysteriously collected unemployment cheques – and ask them a lot of hard questions.

Finally, and inevitably, there was the rumour about Mr Proctor. He was pushing fifty now, and quieter than ever, and unmarried as ever. He wrote how-to books for a living and lived alone in a two-storey frame house that he'd fixed up by himself. Everybody had long assumed he was gay, and as we all know gay people just can't wait to take a knife to straights like us, and so whenever anything notably terrible happened in town, a lot of people looked to Mr Proctor.

I'm told that the Chief also paid Mr Proctor a visit very soon after one of the farm hands discovered Mae Swenson's body.

The department store became another gathering place for yarn-spinners. If the clerks weren't huddling together to tell campfire tales, the clerks and the customers were huddling together. The customers told better stories, especially those who'd had a few drinks. One of them even suggested that eighty-one year old Mae had had a boyfriend –"one of them male strippers from what I hear" – who had killed her because she was breaking up with him.

The horror of the bloody murder lasted most of the morning. But just after lunch, the horror having been dulled somewhat by now, talk turned to Mae Swenson's fabled and fabulous treasure – all that loot, all those diamonds somewhere in her house.

I was wondering about the loot myself.

Josh stopped in around two-thirty that afternoon. "You hear there's a posse combing the woods?"

"I wonder if the Chief knows."

"He's part of it."

"What're they looking for?"

"Nobody's saying."

He paused a moment and said, "You get off at five?"

"Uh-huh."

"I'll meet you at the front door."

"Where we going?"

He stared at me a long and sombre time. "I think we need to talk a little bit about last night."

"The blood?"

"Yeah. The blood."

I looked around the empty shoe department. I wanted to make sure that nobody was within hearing distance.

"I didn't kill her, Josh."

"Maybe not. But I have a feeling you know something about it."

"That's different from killing her."

"Not necessarily. You ever hear of 'accessory after the fact?'"

I forced a smile. "You been watching Court TV again?"

"Yeah. I had to do a paper on it. They spent a whole half hour talking about this guy who'd been charged as 'an accessory after the fact.' He got his ass nailed."

"How bad?"

"Ten to fifteen years."

"Wow."

"Something you should think about, brother."

"I'll see you at five."

But right before five Josh called.

"Coach Beaumont's on the rag again. He doesn't think our practices have been going all that well. So he's making us stay till seven."

"We can talk tonight."

"I'm scared for you, Spence. I really am."

And the way his voice quavered when he said it, I could tell that he really was.

13

Dad said, "I hear there's this nephew."

Mom said, "Nephew?"

We were at the dinner table.

"A nephew who can't hold a job, and who's been in trouble with the law, and who already owed her a lot of money anyway."

"Oh," Mom said, "I heard that one, too. Except it was a niece."

"A niece?"

"Yeah. According to Mrs Finch there was a niece who's a wet T-shirt gal over in Muscatine."

"What's a wet T-shirt gal?"

"You know, goes around to all these taverns where they have wet T-shirt nights, and always wins first prize. But she was always bumming money off Mae, and last night Mae said no, and so the niece killed her."

"The niece", said Dad, "makes a better story than the nephew."

"She sure does," Mom smiled. "Especially the part about the wet T-shirt contests." Then she looked sad. "Poor Mae. Old woman out there all alone, and somebody does something like this to her."

"I'm glad we've got the death penalty back."

To me, Mom said, "I never used to agree with your dad about the death penalty, remember?"

"Uh-huh."

"But now I do. There's some things that people do that are so terrible there's only one way to punish them." She looked sad again. "And this is one of them."

Fifteen minutes later, I was in the upstairs john, brushing my teeth and combing my hair, and getting ready to go out for the evening.

Not that I had any idea where I was going. But I was restless. I just kept seeing poor Mae there on the bed. There weren't any words for what Garrett had done to her.

I heard the phone ring but I let Mom get it. Most of the calls were for her and Josh.

I was just walking to my room when Mom called up the stairs. "For you." Beat. "Cindy Brasher."

A great joy and a great anger and a great panic came over me. I was already trying to contrive a personality for the phone.

Debonair? Not likely for somebody like me.

Glad to hear from her? No, that would sound like I'd eat up any crumbs she was willing to scatter on the ground.

Ominous – hinting that I knew about last night? No; I didn't want to sound like a blackmailer.

I picked up the receiver in my room.

"Hi, Spence."

"Hi."

"Is this a bad time? I mean, are you busy?"

"Not especially. Just getting ready to go out."

"Oh, should I call you back some other time?"

"This is fine."

My heart was threatening to tear out of my chest, like that monster in *Alien* that comes bursting out.

"I wondered if you'd talk to me."

"I thought I was talking to you."

"I mean in person."

"Oh."

"I'd really appreciate it."

"I don't know, Cindy."

"I'm really sorry for the way I treated you."

"Yeah, I'll bet."

"There were things going on, Spence – things I couldn't talk about till now."

I decided to have a little mean fun.

"Boy, that was terrible about Mrs Swenson, wasn't it?"

179

Long pause. "I really need to see you, Spence. Tonight."

"What time?" It felt great to have control of a situation that involved Cindy.

"An hour from now."

"Where?"

"Old Franklin school. The one that burned down?"

"Why there?"

"Somebody's following me, Spence. It's not too far from my house. I can slip out the back way and he won't see me go."

Some more mean fun.

"You sound like you're in trouble, Cindy."

"I don't want to talk on the phone, Spence."

"All right."

"I really appreciate this."

"I'm not going to let you use me again, Cindy."

"I don't blame you for being angry."

"What's Garrett going to think about you seeing me?"

Long pause again. "He's the one who's following me."

"Why?"

"I'll tell you when I see you."

"An hour?"

"An hour. And – thanks, Spence."

An hour from now I was going to see Cindy Brasher again. I didn't even give a damn about the murder anymore. All I could think of was Cindy.

All I could think about was what it would be like to hold her again, and have her whisper those things I carried around with me like fragments of a half, forgotten song.

14

I was just leaving my room when Josh appeared in the doorway.

"We need to talk," he said.

He came in and closed the door and went over and sat on the edge of the bed.

"Somebody saw you," he said.

"Somebody saw me what?"

"Drive away from the Swenson house last night."

"How the hell would you know that?"

"You forget. The Chief's son is on the team."

"Oh."

I leaned against the door. I felt exhausted now. I wanted to crawl into bed and sleep forever. Not even the prospect of Cindy seemed so dazzling.

"They said it was an old brown car."

"There are a lot of old brown cars."

"Not that many."

"Who saw me?"

"Guy Everback. The farmer who lives out near there."

"He say it was me?"

"No, he just said it was an old brown car." He sighed, shook his head. "So you were out there?"

"Yes. But I didn't kill her. She was dead when I got there."

"What the hell were you doing out there?"

"Checking on somebody."

"Checking on somebody? What the hell does that mean?" He got up, started pacing. "This is the kind of thing they execute you for in this state."

"I didn't kill her."

"There was sure a hell of a lot of blood on your clothes last night."

"I know."

"That's all you've got to say? 'I know.'"

"I'm going to take care of it."

"What'd you do with the clothes?"

"Buried them."

"Where?"

"Out by the garage. Under the garbage cans."

"A dog could dig that up."

"Not in winter."

He looked sad now. "You know what this kind of thing would do to Mom and Dad?"

"What 'kind of thing'? I didn't do anything."

"You admit you were out there."

"All right."

"And somebody saw a car like yours pulling away."

"So?"

"And you had bloody clothes on when you came home."

"All right."

"And then you buried them underneath the garbage cans. How do you think all this is going to sound to the Chief?"

I walked over to the window. Looked out. All the roof tops looked familiar, snug and snow-mantled in the night. I'd seen them from this perspective for so many years. Once again, I had the desire to be a boy, and to face nothing more serious than a boy ever faced.

"It's only a matter of time until the Chief starts rounding up everybody in town who has a car like yours."

"By then, I'll have figured it out."

"Figured what out?" Josh said.

"How to turn the real killer over."

He looked startled. "You really know who the killer is?"

"Yes."

"And you haven't told the Chief?"

"Not yet."

"Why?"

"Because — there's somebody I have to help first."

"The only person you should worry about is yourself. This is first-degree murder we're talking here."

"I know. I just need a day or two."

"In a day or two, you could be in jail."

"I'll have to take that chance."

"You're taking too many chances, Spence."

He came over and put his hand on my shoulder. Big brother. Except he was little brother. "I want to help you, Spence. I can talk to the Chief before you do, if that'd help."

"Maybe later. Not now."

"This thing is only going to get worse, Spence."

"I have to go now."

"Maybe I'll go to the Chief myself."

"No!"

I spun around and grabbed him by the front of his shirt. It was kind of funny, me holding him like this. He was so much taller than me.

"No, Josh," I said. "Please. I need a few days, and I need to do this my way. There's somebody innocent involved. I need to help −"

I stopped myself. I'd been about to say "her."

"You need help, Spence. Maybe a psychologist or somebody like that. You could be the prime suspect, man, and you don't even seem to care."

"There's something I have to do first, Josh. You'll just have to trust me."

And with that, I left my room.

15

Something was wrong.

I stood next to the door on the driver's side of my car and saw that it was open by half an inch or so.

Getting it to close took a certain trick, one I'd mastered a long time ago, one I used every time I left the car.

But now the door was open. Somebody had been in here. I did a quick search of the front and back seats but couldn't find anything missing.

All I could think of was what Josh had said about the Chief being told of a car that looked like mine.

Had the Chief decided to check mine out himself? I'd parked, as I usually did, alongside the garage, Josh always parked at the kerb out front, and Dad, to baby the family Buick, always took the garage.

I had some trouble getting the car started. I prayed to the god of old and obstinate motors and he finally came through for me. The engine kicked over.

I was two blocks from my house when I saw Garrett in his police car.

There'd been a fender bender at a stoplight.

Garrett stood by one of the cars, his foot up on the bumper, writing things down in his book. He was wearing his new cowskin western boots.

His Magnum rode his Sam Browne with imposing and impressive majesty. This was what gave Garrett his superiority to all other merely mortal citizens – not his badge, not his officer's oath, but his weapon. And his legal right to use it when he saw fit.

He seemed to sense me. He glanced up just as I slowly entered the intersection. Our eyes met, held.

Only because I started to fishtail a little bit did I look away.

I gripped the wheel and steered the car through the intersection.

Did he know that I was going to see Cindy tonight? Did he know that Cindy had turned to me when she was in the worst trouble of her life?

Heady feelings. That a girl so beautiful would choose me as her confidante.

Garrett no longer scared me.

Soon enough, he'd be in prison for the murder he'd committed last night, and Cindy would be free to see me again.

16

My mom and dad went to Franklin back in the days when school officials around here still tried to ban Elvis records from being played at dances.

Mom always talks about how girls wore saddle-shoes and petticoats and ponytails. Dad always talks about how boys wore black leather jackets and engineering boots and rode around in hot rods.

To be honest, it's kind of hard to imagine either one of my parents as 'cool' kids. I keep trying to imagine them as 'cool' kids but I can never quite finish painting the picture. And the photos they've shown me from time to time make them look as nerdy as I was in high school. Maybe that's the difference. I always knew I was a nerd. Maybe Mom and Dad were blissfully ignorant. Or maybe the entire class was nerdy and so Mom and Dad fit in just fine.

In the moonlight, Franklin school stood dark and solemn and gutted, the char black and char grey of the fire that destroyed it still clinging to the two brick walls left standing.

Against the snow, the building had a kind of ugly beauty.

I parked my car a block away and took the alley so that nobody would see me pull up.

I crunched across the snow leading to the school. Overhead, above the clouds, I heard a jet roar across the prairie sky, leaving a plume of glowing white exhaust that angled across the full moon.

A collie came around the corner of the building, sniffing the ground for buried treasure. When he saw me, he swung away, heading across the open field behind the school.

No sign of Cindy.

I walked around the entire building, then carefully picked my way through the tumbledown inside. As children, we'd always been warned against playing in here. A small boy had fallen into a shallow hole soon after the fire, and had had his arm amputated as a result.

Cindy must have fallen down a hole. Still no sign of her.

I stood in the windless night staring at the brick building, trying to imagine the sounds of early Elvis records pouring from the open windows on a soft spring afternoon. And somewhere inside would be my parents, dancing in their petticoats and duck's-ass haircut.

"I'm sorry I'm late."

When I turned, I saw her walking toward me from the alley. She'd taken the same route I had.

She wore a red parka and jeans. The parka hood framed her face and made her more beautiful than ever. I couldn't help it. At that moment I didn't care about anything except being with her.

I walked over to her.

Neither of us said anything, just slid our arms around each other and came together in a kiss.

"We'd better hide," she said, after a time.

Inside the burned out building, we found a niche of clean brick where we could sit down next to each other. It was cold there but I didn't care.

She said, "I told him."

"About what?"

"About us. Tonight. Meeting."

"What?" I looked at her as I would at a small child who'd just admitted doing something horrible. "Why would you do that?"

"He made me."

"God, Cindy."

"He stopped over at the house. Right after dinner. I didn't expect him. He got me alone in my room and — and he knew that I was holding something back from him."

"So you told him about us?"

"Don't you understand, Spence, I didn't have any choice? He'd already figured it out for himself anyway. He's a very jealous guy — he's still jealous of David and David's dead. So you can imagine how he is about you."

I was angry enough to forget romance momentarily. I said, "You were with him when he killed Mae Swenson the other night."

She slipped her parka hood off. In the moonlight through the broken school window, I could see the fine lines of her face and the nervous beauty of her eyes.

"I tried to tell you before, Spence. But you wouldn't listen."

"Tell me what?"

"About the well."

"Dammit, Cindy, that's just a game you invented. There's nothing down that well."

She looked shocked, then hurt, then angry. "You think you know so much. You admit you heard something the night we were out there."

"The power of suggestion, Cindy. That's all it was."

"Well, David heard something. And so did Garrett."

"The same thing. Suggestion."

I couldn't stand the way she glared at me now, hating me.

I took her hand. At first, she tried to tug it away but finally she let its slender, tender warmth rest in my hand.

"Cindy, I talked to a shrink the other day."

"About what?'

"About the well."

"Oh. I'm sure he said I was crazy. Especially since I've already been in the hospital and everything."

"That isn't what he said at all."

We were silent for a time.

She said, "What did he say?"

"He called it Shared Psychotic Disorder."

"What does that mean?"

"Just that when one person imagines something and he shares it with somebody else, then that person imagines the same thing. And then they both begin believing it's true, even when it's not."

"I hate shrinks."

"He's a pretty nice guy."

"When I was in the mental hospital, one of them was always feeling me up."

"You should've reported him."

"They would've said I was crazy is all, and imagining things. Like this Psychotic Disorder you're talking about."

As gently as I could, I said, "That's what's happening with the well, Cindy. You imagine things, but you imagine it so vividly that you get other people imagining things too."

"David did what the thing in the well told him to do. He killed that clerk at the convenience store."

I sighed, said nothing.

"And Garrett did just what the alien told him to do, too. He killed Mrs Swenson."

"You didn't have anything to do with killing either one of them."

"It wouldn't have happened if I hadn't brought them to the well," she said.

"If the alien makes people kill, then why haven't you killed anybody?"

"That isn't what he wants me to do."

"I see."

Angry: "Don't fucking talk to me like that! That's how everybody talked to me when I got out of the mental hospital. 'Now, now dear, don't get yourself excited.'"

Her voice was loud and harsh on the prairie night. The collie heard her and swung back for another look. He stood at

189

where the entrance of the school had been and watched us for a long minute or two.

"I'm sorry."

"All right. Apology accepted."

Then: "All it wants me to do is bring boys to the well. That's my only part in it."

"But you went along with Garrett to Swenson's."

"He made me. He said he'd kill me if I didn't."

"You took me to the well. I didn't kill anybody."

"I think it has to do with innocence."

"I'm not exactly innocent."

"But you don't hate – you're not angry."

"And David and Garrett –"

"Rage. Most of the time, anyway. I think the alien can use that. It makes it easier for it to take control of them."

This was all insane but I had to be very careful not to let her think that that was what I was thinking.

"Did you see Garrett kill the woman?"

"Yes."

"So you could testify against him in court?'

"Yes." Pause. "But I'm just as guilty as he is, don't you see that? He wouldn't have done it if I hadn't brought him to the well."

I took her shoulder and turned her face full to mine.

"I want you to understand one thing, Cindy. These murders have got you so upset that you're blaming yourself. You didn't have anything to do with them."

"So you don't believe that there's an alien in that well?"

"I'm saying the alien doesn't matter."

"Then what matters?'

"That Myles and Garrett each chose to kill somebody."

"But they wouldn't have without me."

"Did you *tell* David to shoot the clerk?"

"Well, no."

"Did you tell Garrett to stab Mae Swenson?"

190

"No."

"Then you're not guilty of *anything*, Cindy."

Long pause. "You don't believe me about the well."

"I guess I haven't made my mind up yet."

"It's down there."

"Say I believe you. For the sake of argument. It's not going to make any difference in a court of law, is it?"

She looked confused.

"David killed the clerk and Garrett killed Mae Swenson, right?"

"Right."

"Well, that's all the court is going to care about."

"But I should testify about the well."

"You know how people talked to you when you got out of the mental hospital?"

"Real patronising and all?"

"Exactly. Well, if you sat in the witness stand and tried to tell the court about the well, that's how people would treat you again."

"You think they'd send me back to the mental hospital?"

"Possibly."

"I'd rather die than go back to that hospital. That doctor really did feel me up all the time. And one time I woke up after he gave me a lot of drugs and my vagina was really sore. I think he raped me."

"That's why you don't want to tell anybody else about the well – and you sure as hell wouldn't want to tell the court. You see?"

"I don't want to go back to the mental hospital."

"Then let me handle it."

She stared at me. "What're you going to do?"

"I'm not sure yet. But don't tell anybody about the well. Or that you were out at Swenson's that night."

It was going to work out. I would ask the Chief to investigate Garrett, and then, after the trial was over and Garrett found guilty, Cindy and I would be free to be together.

"Cindy, I love you," I said.

"I love you, too, Spence."

When we were kissing there in the burned-out shell of the building, the winter night wondrously golden in the moonlight, a distant freight train lonely on the darkness, I felt exhilarated about what lay ahead for me.

Cindy lay ahead for me.

Cindy my girlfriend, Cindy my wife.

Richard Mitchell, KNAX-TV:

"Even in the rain, the anti-capital punishment group continues to march in protest in front of the prison gates. A man beats a drum that makes a lonely, chilling sound in the darkness tonight. You have to wonder if the condemned prisoner can hear that drum in the death chamber. There are only a few minutes to go now, a few more minutes before a human life is snuffed in retribution for a horrible crime. Listen to that terrible lonely drum sound in the night, just listen to it."

Tape 40-D, December 2. Interview between Attorney Risa Wiggins and her client in the Clark County jail.

A: That was the night you set fire to the well?

C: Yeah. I figured if I dumped enough gasoline down there and set a fire, maybe that would get rid of the alien.

A: Did it?

C: I thought it did. For a few days, anyway. But then the chanting in my head started again. (Pause) I don't think anything can kill that alien. I think it's indestructible. You know, just like in the Sci-Fi movies. I mean, they could drop a nuclear bomb on it and it wouldn't make any difference.

17

I took Cindy home in a circuitous way through alleys so that Garrett wouldn't have a chance to see us.

"I'm afraid of going back to the mental hospital, Spence."

"You're not going back to the mental hospital."

"Garrett'll say I made him do it."

I looked over at her and smiled. "Nobody'll believe that, Cindy."

"But the well."

"Remember the Shared Psychotic Disorder?"

"Then you don't believe there's an alien in the well?"

"There isn't one, Cindy."

"Then you're saying I'm crazy?"

"I'm saying that you have a great imagination. So do I."

"I really hear stuff down that well."

"I heard stuff that one night myself," I said.

"But you still think it was just your imagination?"

"Absolutely."

"I'm still worried about prison."

I reached across and took her hand. "I'm going to the Chief and tell him everything, Cindy. He'll believe me and then he'll arrest Garrett."

"You really think it can be that easy?"

We had just reached her garage. Moonlight painted her back yard a glowing gold colour.

"I love you, Cindy."

She leaned over and kissed me.

"Thanks for believing me, that I didn't have anything to do with the murders I mean."

"I'll talk to you tomorrow."

When I got home, I spent a few minutes talking to my folks and then I went upstairs to my room.

I was just reaching for the light switch when I noticed a flash in the back yard where I'd parked my car next to the alley.

Somebody was down there with a flashlight.

I went to my bureau and got my binoculars.

I expected to see Garrett down there.

At first, I couldn't see anything, just darkness, a dark human form leaning into the back seat of my car.

No police vehicle was any place in sight.

Then I let my eyes adjust to the binoculars and to the darkness.

The figure finally finished in the back seat and stood erect outside my car again.

It was the Chief.

He was holding something almost delicately in his hand. He took some kind of plastic bag from the pocket of his parka and lovingly, carefully slid the object inside there.

I couldn't see what the object was.

But I knew what the plastic carrier was: an evidence bag. They get tagged with a letter and a number and are used in court when the prosecutor is trying to trail the defendant to the wall.

All I could think of was how my car door had been slightly ajar when I'd gone out tonight.

All I could think of was that somebody had seen my car out at the Swenson place.

A knock came behind me.

I turned around and saw Josh silhouetted in the doorway.

"You got a minute?" he said. Then, nodding to the binoculars, "What's going on?"

"Chief's down at my car."

"Oh."

His reaction was odd. I'd expected him to be excited or upset when I told him about the Chief.

He said, "That's what I wanted to talk to you about."

"Oh?"

"Mind if I turn the light on and close the door? I don't want Mom and Dad to hear this."

"To hear what?"

But he didn't answer my question. He clipped on the light, shut the door, and came over and sat down on my desk chair. I sat on the edge of the bed.

"One of the guys on the team has a cousin who works at the police station," Josh said.

"So?" His mysteriousness was beginning to irritate me.

"So, he told me that the Chief got this anonymous note this afternoon."

That was the first time I felt fear. You know how it is — suddenly your bowels turn queasy, and your hands begin to twitch, and you sense that terrible trouble lies just ahead?

"What did the note say?" I tried to act as if I was holding up just fine but I think Josh could see that I was scared.

"Said you killed Mae Swenson."

"Oh, shit," I said.

"Yeah. That's what I say."

"I didn't kill her, Josh. I swear I didn't. And Cindy can testify to that." I told him what Cindy had said about Garrett.

He got up abruptly, clipped off the light and walked to the window again. He picked up my binoculars and put them to his eyes.

"The Chief's gone," he said. "I wonder what the hell he was looking for."

"He found something," I said. "In the back seat. He put it in one of those evidence bags."

Josh shook his head and set down the binoculars. He went back and sat at the desk chair. He didn't bother to turn on the lights.

"Maybe you should talk to Mom and Dad."

"What would I say?"

"Say what you said to me."

"Everything?"

"Yeah, everything."

"They won't know how to handle it, Josh."

"They're stronger people than you think, Spence. They really are. You probably need an attorney right now. Dad knows a couple of good ones in town here."

I got up and started pacing, gaping out the window every few seconds, half-expecting to see the Chief down there again.

"Should I tell them about the well?"

"I guess," he said. "But I sure wouldn't say you believe there's something down there."

"I talked to a shrink about that."

"Yeah?"

I told him about Shared Psychotic Disorder.

"I'm glad you had that talk. I was starting to worry about you."

I paced some more.

He just watched me.

I kept thinking that the Chief could never actually suspect me. I wasn't the killer type. I was this harmless kid who read a lot of Sci-Fi paperbacks and served in the Army and then came back home to settle into adulthood. I guess most of us think that way – that most people see each of us as innocents who couldn't do anything that was terribly wrong, that they see that overall we're good, decent people just like they are. But for the first time, I wondered if that was true. Maybe that wasn't how people perceived me at all. Maybe they saw me as sinister in some way, maybe they wouldn't have any trouble at all seeing me as a murderer.

But I kept seeing him bent into the back seat there, retrieving something. And putting it into an evidence bag.

"This is gonna be hard, Josh. Telling Mom and Dad."

"You better do it before the Chief does."

"I guess that's a good point."

"She's got to tell the truth."

"She?"

"Cindy Brasher."

"Oh."

"She's got to go to the Chief and tell him exactly what happened."

"She's afraid of being sent back to the mental hospital."

"Tough shit, Spence. This is your life we're talking about here."

I went to the window, looked out again. The snow was blue now that the moon had disappeared behind the clouds, that winter night blue that is the wan colour of an alien landscape,

Downstairs, the doorbell rang.

"Shit," I said.

"What?"

"It's late for company."

"Yeah, I guess you're right."

"Would you go down and see who it is?"

He stood up and came over to me and took me roughly by the arm. "You've got to get control of yourself, Spence. You understand?"

I did understand.

I took several deep breaths.

His big hand was still cinched on my arm.

I guess he could see that I was calming down.

"I'll be back up right away."

"Thanks, Josh."

"Just keep control of yourself."

"I will. I promise."

"This thing is going to come out all right. It really will."

I knew he'd said that just to make me feet better but I appreciated it.

From downstairs, I could hear the faint rumble of voices. Mom and Dad talking to the visitor.

He gave me a buck-up hit on the arm and then left my room.

I went back to the window and looked out.

Night is so different from day. Two completely separate

worlds. That's why vampires always made sense to me. They're truly creatures of the night.

It seemed like a hour, waiting there for Josh.

He came up the stairs very, very slowly. Usually he bounds up them two at a time. I knew this was a bad sign. Walking slowly mean that he was reluctant to give me bad news.

He came into the room and stood there for a moment looking at me.

My bowels went cold and my heart started hammering so hard, it scared me.

"The Chief's downstairs talking to Mom and Dad," he said. Then he paused a really long time. "I guess he did find something in your car tonight."

"What?"

"A knife."

"Oh, God."

"With blood all over it."

"Garrett planted it. That sonofabitch."

"The Chief thinks it's the murder weapon."

I felt as bad for Mom and Dad as I did for me. I couldn't imagine what they must be feeling right now – terror, fear, embarrassment – the Chief standing there and implying that perhaps their son was a killer.

"The Chief would like you to come down."

"All right."

"Right away, he said."

"I'll be down. just give me a minute. I need to go to the john." And I did. My body felt as if it were starting to run amuck, organ by organ. I couldn't think clearly at all. Reality seemed to be lost behind a wispy fog of horror.

"You really should come down."

"Just tell him I needed to go to the john."

Josh nodded. "We're going to fight this, Spence."

He didn't sound nearly as positive as he had right before he'd gone downstairs.

Then he surprised me by coming over and hugging me. I almost cried. I really did. Because I felt in the hug not only brotherly affection but fear. After seeing the Chief, Josh was as frightened for me as I was.

I spent a quick minute in the john and then hurried back to my room.

I had to move quickly.

Before the Chief got curious and came upstairs.

I stuffed a scarf, gloves, and hunting knife into my jacket. I slipped my jeans off and slipped on a pair of long johns then tugged on my jeans again. I put on one of my heavy Army sweaters. I even put on those old lace-up hunting boots that I'd inherited from Dad.

I was warm as I could be and still remain ambulatory.

Raising the window without making any noise was difficult. I had to raise it a quarter-inch at a time.

As I eased it up, I could feel the cold night air slipping into the house.

In a strange way, the cold air felt good, almost inviting. I was going to be one of those night creatures now. Running for my life. The way so many of the comic books and paperbacks had depicted the lives of their heroes, misunderstood people hunted by stupid and vicious mobs.

I raised the window only as high as absolutely necessary, and then I pushed myself through the opening and stood on the snow-laden roof of the back porch.

I dropped to the ground, the shock to my knees considerable, despite the snowfall.

Then I started running.

I didn't know what else to do.

All I could think of was the bloody knife the Chief had found. Pretty convincing evidence. He'd mark me guilty and not listen to anything I had to say.

I couldn't let that happen. I couldn't.

Part Three

1

After a time, I was beyond pain. I slipped and fell so many times, hurt so many parts of my body, landing on hands and knees torn raw, that I became numb.

I had no idea where I was going.

To reach the edge of town, I took a succession of alleys. The sight of chimney smoke had a sentimental effect on me. I thought of all the lucky people in those snug little houses. I envied them, and in a way I even hated them. They'd believe what the Chief told them to believe. They'd think I was guilty. They'd say, Oh, yes, he always was a strange boy. I guess I ain't exactly surprised he killed old Mae.

I ran.

When I reached the edge of town, I swung over to the rail yards. The half mile or so of double-track box cars hid me pretty well.

I thought of swinging myself up into one of the cars and hiding there for a time. But the rail yard was probably one of the first places they'd look. Freight trains came in twenty-four hours a day. They'd probably figure I'd hop one.

Then I ran down empty gravel roads that cut between fallow cornfields covered with midnight blue snow. The harder I ran, the more dream-like it all seemed to me. I saw a hawk glide down the moonbeams, and I was so touched by its majestic loneliness that I almost cried. I didn't want to escape on a box car. I wanted to escape on the back of a hawk, have him take me to one of the faraway lands I read about in my paperbacks.

A car came rumbling up over the hill behind me.

I pitched myself straight down into the ravine. More pain. I barely felt it.

I crawled around until I came to a shallow culvert. I scampered in there, my hands feeling broken glass, dead weeds, gnarled cigarette packs, and the hard dried pebble-like faeces of rats and rabbits.

The car came down the road. I could feel the vibrations in the concrete of the culvert.

It seemed to slow as it drew closer. I had an image of the Chief's car, Garrett sitting next to him with a shotgun, winking at each other. They knew where I was but they were going to be coy about it. They'd slow down a little right here to scare me but then they'd go on, as if they didn't suspect anything at all, and then they'd stop about a quarter mile down the road, just pull off on to the shoulder the way pheasant hunters do in the autumn, and then start their trek back for me.

The car rolled on.

I listened to its weight and rumble recede into the night. What if it was the Chief? What if he was just trying to trick me?

I was already tired of the culvert. I was scrunched up inside almost foetally, the damned thing was so small.

I had a terrible moment of claustrophobia. What if I couldn't get out of here? What if I was stuck?

I forced myself out of the culvert and back into the night.

Where to go?

In the morning, a road like this would be heavily travelled with trucks bringing milk to market. Somebody was bound to see me.

I started running again. All I could think of was that Cindy would tell the Chief the truth and the manhunt would be called off.

This time I didn't fall. I felt sure-footed in a way I never had before in my entire life.

My feet crunched through snow and ice. My eyes roamed the vast blue-white fields that stretched to the moon itself. My breathing came deep and natural, as if my lungs were adjusting to this pace, even though I'd rarely exercised since coming home from the Army. The cold, far from stinging me, balmed me. I felt one with winter the way a wolf must.

I ran.

When I finally collapsed after four or five miles, I began to wonder what Josh and my parents were doing right now.

I doubted they were asleep. Sleep was going to be impossible for them tonight. For many nights, probably.

Even though I'd done nothing to bring on my fate, I hated myself for making them suffer for me. They were good and decent and true people.

I thought of suicide. Maybe that would be best for everybody. No more struggle, no more shame.

The trouble was, I wasn't suicidal. I was one of those people who'd be screaming for life right up to my last breath.

When I finally began to look around, I realised that I was standing in a beaten old deserted barn that sat directly above the line shack and the well in the timberland below.

I walked out into the empty barnyard and looked down into the timber.

Down there. Cindy and that crazy obsession of hers.

Alien beings.

Shared Psychotic Disorder.

I had my place for the night.

In one of the horse stalls, I found an ancient dusty horse blanket that didn't smell too badly of horseshit, and I draped myself in it, and I parked my butt in the deepest darkest corner of the stall, and stayed there until dawn, when a plump mother raccoon appeared at the head of the stall and started staring at me.

Her gaze woke me. I sensed it – and her on some kind of pure animal level.

I wished I had something for her to eat. I wanted to show her I was friendly.

I wanted to pet her the way you would a cat. I needed that animal warmth and love.

I moved as carefully as I could.

Maybe she wouldn't spook and run away.

But spook and run away, she did.

I felt spurned, as if a lover had walked out on me. I wanted to plead with the raccoon to come back. She was a mother, she could mother me.

Then, slowly, I realised that fear and lack of good sleep had made me more than a little crazed.

She wasn't a human being, she was a raccoon, and she hadn't spurned me, she'd simply done what raccoons do when they encounter species larger than themselves – run away.

I stood up and walked down to the open barn door and took my morning piss.

The dawn sky was grey and low. The colour had been blanched out of everything. It was like looking at a black and white photo.

I went back to the barn for the horse blanket and set it on a piece of tumbledown fence to let it air out for a while.

Then I heard them.

Voices.

Coming up the hill through the timber.

The Chief.

Running away as I had, the Chief was sure to use a posse to find me. They never use that word anymore, 'posse' – they call them 'concerned citizens' now or something like that – but that's what these men were.

A posse with guns and mean intent.

I ran out to the blanket and brought it back inside. I didn't want any signs of me hanging out there for them to see.

I had to make a quick decision.

I could hide here, probably up in the hay mow, and maybe they wouldn't find me, and I'd be safe for a day or so till they doubled-back to some of the places they'd covered before.

But I'd have a better chance running.

I looked at the horse blanket. It might be the only thing I'd find to keep me warm tonight.

Take it with me?

No, it'd be too bulky to carry, and if I was forced to drop it somewhere, they'd find it and be able to track my course.

I reluctantly pitched the blanket into the corner of the stall and then I went to the far eastern door of the barn, the one that pointed away from the timber, and even higher up into the hills.

I got outside and then I did the only thing I could do.

I ran.

2

I spent the stern grey morning running across ice-hard creeks
and working my way through rough stands of birch and
dragging myself up hills, even though all my stamina was gone.

I had a desperate idea for escape. I would work my way all
the way up into the hills and then double back to the west,
eventually working my way down to the line shack and Cindy's
well.

Close to noon, I heard the angry barking of hunting dogs,
followed by two quick shots.

Obviously, somebody thought they'd found me.

I kept on moving, staying to trees because somebody might
see me from one of the county roads.

A couple of times, I dropped to my knees and just stayed
there for long, gasping minutes. I was tired, hungry, confused,
scared.

I hadn't killed anybody yet there was a good chance I'd lose
my life either in the electric chair or by a bullet from one of the
posse members. Not for nothing does this kind of man carry a
shotgun rack in the back windows of his pick-up, daydreaming
of the day his prey isn't a deer but is instead a real live human
being – one he'll soon make dead.

Then voices sounded on the air like gunshots. A small group
of them had apparently fanned out west.

The dogs were barking loudly and incessantly now. They
must have scented me.

I ran. I didn't know what else to do. There was no place to
hide.

I ran until I came to a shabby little acreage with a shack for
a house and some sad scrawny chickens eating silage corn from
the snowy ground.

An old woman in longjohns and an apron and men's hunting
boots walked the chicken yard, dispersing the corn from a sack.
She was a throwback. There hadn't been pioneer women like

her – hard, and often more resilient than their male counterparts – in almost a century now, not since the Oklahoma land rush.

She didn't see me on the far side of her garage.

I peered in through a grimy window.

A twenty-five year old Plymouth sat there, buff blue with jet wings and a few hundred pounds of chrome. The last era when America strode the world like a Colossus.

My first guess was that the damned thing probably didn't run but then I saw the tyre tracks running from the road to the garage.

The dogs were closer, louder now, just back of the rise.

I eased over to the side door of the garage and snuck inside. I had to move quickly.

I had an idea for fooling the dogs. Might work, might not. I didn't have a hell of a lot of choice at the moment.

The garage smelled of car oil, a lawnmower bag's dead summer grass, cat piss, and ancient water-soaked lumber.

The garage was small. I had to squeeze my way to the back of the car.

I found a small coil of wire on a hook, took it down, and proceeded to work on the trunk lock.

I had no idea what I was doing. Burglary had never appealed to me before.

I jimmied that lock for a good five minutes, all the time the dogs growing louder and louder, nearer and nearer.

And then – voilà – it popped open.

This was not a testament to my skills. The rusted lock had simply surrendered to the wiggling and waggling piece of wire. Twenty-five-year-old locks have a tendency to do that.

I got in the trunk and pulled the lid down.

Darkness.

The smell of new rubber. I blindly felt the tread of a new spare tyre.

By now, I had so many cuts, nicks, and bruises that huddling inside the trunk wasn't even especially uncomfortable.

If I hadn't had to pee, I wouldn't have been uncomfortable at all.

I waited.

A few minutes later, I heard the men and the dogs reach the acreage.

They shouted hellos to the old woman and she shouted a hello back, her voice as hard as their own.

The dogs must have scented me because their barking increased. Maybe I'd dropped something that they were now focusing on.

I heard the woman say, "I sure hope you catch that little bastard. Mae Swenson was a good friend of mine. And if you do find him, do me a favour and kill him right on the spot."

The dogs kept barking but they didn't move any closer to the garage.

Just as I'd hoped, they could not scent me through both the wall of the garage and the metal of the car trunk.

The men moved away then, the barking receding on the stillness as they moved higher into the hills.

Then silence.

Needing to piss. The smell of rubber. My breath still coming in hard sweaty gasps.

Do me a favour and kill him right on the spot.

Don't bother to find out if he's really guilty.

Don't bother to listen to his side of things.

Even as a little boy, I'd always had that fear of groups of people. Whenever I approached them, I sensed that they were a unit, one that would never include me, one that could turn on me and take my life because I was not like them.

A long time later, I opened the trunk.

It squeaked.

I froze.

What if the old woman was still in the yard?

But no, at least an hour had passed since the posse had

been here.

The old woman would be inside.

I opened the trunk even more, so I could look out through the dirty window of the garage.

The sky was even more overcast now. And snow was starting to fall. The snow would help me. The dogs wouldn't be able to track me as well through snowfall.

Then she was there, in the window, glaring at me.

She had an old-fashioned Colt .45 in her hand and it was pointed right at me.

"You come out of there," she said, "and if you make a move I don't like, I'm going to kill you on the spot. You understand?"

I understood.

I came out of there.

I tried real hard not to make a move she didn't like.

3

The interior of the shack was an explosion of dusty overstuffed furniture, knickknacks, piles of aged magazines, a kitchen that smelled of rancid grease, and a living room that was just big enough to contain a black and white television console that had been new before I was born. The prize piece was the purple velveteen recliner. Next to it was a wobbly pressed wood end table upon which sat a glass and a bottle of Old Grandad. And next to the bottle were two small ceramic coffee mugs, one a Jack O'Lantern, one a Santa Claus. She was ready for any holiday you cared to push at her.

My claustrophobia was back. Not only did the oppressive clutter get to me, so did the sense of the life lived here – the life of a hardscrabble isolated packrat. In my romantic world, people shouldn't live this way.

She waggled her Colt .45 at me.

"Hands up."

"I didn't kill her."

"Shit," she said. "If you didn't kill her, why'd they find that knife in your car?"

"Somebody put it there."

"Shit." Then: "She was one of the few friends I had." Her tears were quick and plentiful, softening the hard lined face into a semblance of beauty. You could see the young woman she'd been. A sad strange history had probably led her to this shack.

"I'm sorry she's dead."

She snuffled tears. "You're sorry for yourself. Sorry you're on the run, and sorry they'll put you to death up at the state prison. That's who you're sorry for."

There was a black dial telephone, much older even than her TV set, sitting on the far arm of the couch.

"If you move, I'll kill you."

"I know. You told me that already."

214

"I could probably get away with it, just sending you over right here and now. Self-defence. And who could prove it wasn't?"

The queasy coldness seized my bowels again.

"Could you not point that at me?"

"You think I don't know how to handle this?"

"I'm sure you do, ma'am. But it could still go off accidentally."

"Can that 'ma'am' shit. I hate it."

She walked backward across the living room to the far edge of the couch. Then she eased herself down and with her empty hand lifted the receiver.

"They should have operators the way they did when I was a girl. All you had to do was say 'Mavis, get me Mrs Mally' and ten seconds later Mavis would have you connected."

She leaned over awkwardly. She had to hold the gun in one hand and with the other dial O.

I had already figured out my last best hope. If I could pick up the Santa Claus mug fast enough, and throw it hard enough, there was a chance I could jump her and tie her up.

She leaned further, as if she were doing some kind of hip exercise, and that was when I grabbed the mug and hurled it at her.

When she yelped, I felt sorry for her. I'd thrown harder than I'd intended, and the mug caught her in the eyebrow.

She fired but by that time, I was ducking down and charging at her.

I tackled her, grabbing her hips, slamming her back into the couch, snatching the gun from her hand.

For a long moment, we just sat there, me in her lap like a favourite grandchild, both of us panting, the air harsh with gunsmoke.

"You're bleeding," I said.

"Screw yourself."

"God, I didn't mean to hurt you."

"I been hurt a lot worse than that." She looked beyond me

215

a moment, and I could tell she was staring down the long corridor of time. "Lost my husband and two babies in a car accident. I was in the hospital for eleven months."

"I'm sorry, ma'am."

The sentiment was gone from her eyes now. She was once more the hard prairie loner. "What'd I tell you about that 'ma'am' shit?"

"Excuse me."

I got up, gripping her .45 in my right hand as I did so. "I'll have to do some things I don't want to do."

"Like what?"

"Like tie you up and tear your phone cord out."

"And you say you didn't kill her."

"I didn't. But nobody believes me so I don't have much choice except to act like I'm guilty."

She didn't look especially swayed by my argument.

There was some clothesline rope on the kitchen sink. I cut off two long pieces and went back and got her wrists and feet tied. Then I went over and ripped the phone cord out of the plug.

"There's one more thing," I said.

Before she could ask what it was, I went into the tiny toilet, which smelled surprisingly sweet — some kind of lilac perfume — and a few moments later I was leaning over her with a Band-Aid and a bottle of iodine and a clean hot soapy wash cloth.

"What the hell you doing?"

"I'm going to clean out your cut from where I hit you.

"Don't bother."

"I didn't mean to hurt you."

She watched me in a kind of disbelief as I treated her small wound.

"You're crazy, you know that?" she said.

"Look who's talking."

When I finished up, the Band-Aid too big for the job and giving her an injured look that was at least a little bit comic, she said, "You really didn't kill her?"

"I really didn't kill her."

"Then who did?"

"A guy named Garrett."

"The cop who works for the Chief?"

"Right."

"Why would a cop kill Mae?"

"I don't have time to explain. But he killed her all right." I went to the window, looked out past dusty red curtains. "When's the next time you're expecting somebody?"

"Tonight, I guess. Why?"

"I just want to make sure you'll be all right."

She stared at me a long moment. "Kid, I sure as hell don't know what to make of you."

I smiled bleakly. "Sometimes I don't know what to make of me, either."

I stepped out of the living room, into the narrow little room where the sleeping cot lay. I picked up the comforter and brought it back to the couch and spread it over her.

"Don't want you to get cold," I said.

I took a last peek at her wound. "Headache?"

"Not any more."

"Good. Your eyes look fine. I didn't give you a concussion or anything."

"A lot of them men looking for you, you know they'll kill you the minute they see you."

"I know."

"Aren't you scared?"

"I can't tell you how scared."

"So you're gonna keep running?"

"I don't have any choice."

I went to the window, looked out again. The sky was greyer and lower than before. There was no sign of the men but overhead, in the distance, I could hear the choppers. That meant they'd brought in the state police to help with the search.

217

I needed to head for the timber. Fast.

"I'll get your gun back to you some way," I said. "I'm sorry to have to take it."

She nodded to the kitchen. "On top of the refrigerator's a box of bullets. Take 'em, kid."

"God, that's really nice of you."

"And inside the refrigerator's a couple of bologna sandwiches. With mustard and mayo. That's how I fix 'em. Take them, too. I can make more for myself."

"That's damned nice of you."

And for the very first time, I saw her smile, and it took forty years from her face. "Yeah, it is, isn't it?" Then, the smile quickly gone: "You better hit the timber fast."

I got the bullets and the sandwiches and went to the door.

"Sorry for hitting you with the mug."

Another long look from her. "Take care of yourself, kid. I guess now I really don't think you did kill Mae." I felt good about having her blessing as I closed her door behind me, and started running for the timberline.

4

I spent the afternoon backtracking.

It was still my intention to get back to the line shack and the well. There was a pay phone on the northernmost edge of the nearby state park. After dark, I could call Mom and Dad and let them know that I was all right.

Late in the afternoon, a soft snow fell, giving the grim grey day a needed grace note.

A few times, cold snowflakes touching my nose and cheeks, I was even able to forget about Mae Swenson. I was a kid again, sledding or making snowmen or tucked into the corner of my bed with a *Werewolf At Night* comic.

But then I'd hear the distant drum of semis on the road that ran parallel to my course, and I'd be reminded again of reality.

Darkness came by five that afternoon. By now, the snowfall had lost its allure. There was enough of it to make walking difficult.

Far, far away, I saw the lights of the town, my town, and for a moment it had the quality of a nightmare. I'd always had dreams of being driven out of society, seeing people whom I cared for wanting nothing to do with me, passing me by on the street with only scorn and malice in their gazes. In these nightmares, I'd never known what my sin was, only that people no longer deemed me worthy of their friendship. And eventually, I began to believe them, to feel that I was unworthy, and so, much as I was doing now, I fled into a dark forest where I hid from the disapproving stare of society.

A couple of times, I was tempted to eat the sandwiches the old woman had given me but I stopped myself.

I envisioned a feast tonight. On the one hand, it was almost laughable. Bologna sandwiches and the leaky roof of a line shack do not a feast make. On the other hand, it made sense. I'd been on the run for the better part of a night and day now. I needed to stop, rest. The line shack was a good place because the posse had probably covered it several times already, different groups criss-crossing it at different points in the search, and so I'd probably be safe.

Safe – and with two bologna sandwiches, complete with mustard and mayo, to complete my feast.

An hour later, the sky cleared.

There was an icy quarter moon. I reached the top of a hill and looked down on the town again.

This time, the haze having lifted, it was postcard pretty, all church steeples and smoking chimneys and the first bright decorations for Christmas. The sentimental quality of the scene only made my sense of loss cut deeper.

I reached the line shack just as two raccoons were leaving it. They watched me for a moment, seeming neither particularly interested in me or afraid, and then waddled away into the snow and the night.

I found a nice dry corner in the shack and sat down. All I did for the first half hour was let myself drift in and out of a frenzied sleep.

I am running down a long endless blacktop road and right behind me are four cop cars with screaming sirens and men leaning out the windows with shotguns.

I am up in my room and I am ten years old and I'm reading my first Leigh Brackett paperback and I doze off and I have this real weird dream about being twenty-one and being accused of murder.

I am dancing across a glass floor sparkling as black diamonds and in my arms is gorgeous, tender, vulnerable Cindy Brasher. Her hair is wind-caught, drifting like golden seaweed in this ocean of perfect night. She wears a gown of impossible glowing ivory, a gown that flatters her soft white skin and lovely face.

The music is beautiful but it is the kind of beauty that is not without the price of melancholy – and so I watch Cindy's face as every few minutes sadness touches then flees her eyes. And then we're one again, and dancing on.

I am twenty-four years old and I am being strapped to a gurney. This is an execution chamber. There are three men in there with me. They don't seem to notice me. They simply go about their business. I scream but it is a silent scream. I pray but there is no God to hear me. The needle, sharp and silver and shining, descends.

I am –

I am twenty-one years and sitting in a line shack and freezing my ass off.

I possess a bladder that needs emptying, a belly that needs food, and a soul that needs peace.

I get up and take care of my bladder first, just outside the empty doorway. I wash my hands in the snow and then I come back in and take care of my belly.

The bologna sandwiches turn out to be a feast. No steak, no lobster, no fancy French gourmet meal ever tasted better.

I am so happy to be eating that even the occasional piece of gristle in the meat has a certain sumptuousness to it.

When I am finished, after having licked every crumb from the waxed paper, I put my head back and doze off again.

And then it happens.

Very quickly, really.

The noise from the well that I heard that first night, the noise that is probably a voice whose words I can't quite make out, a rumbling ominous frightening voice that seems somehow both ancient and unworldly.

I am on my feet –

I am moving toward the door –

I am walking out into the freezing winter night. The voice is

clearer now, rumbling, rumbling just below my hearing –
    I am moving inexorably to the well –
    – the well
    – and what waits for me in the well –

The dream scared the shit out of me.

I wasn't hearing voices.

I wasn't up on my feet.

In the tumbledown silence of the line shack, I sat huddled and trembling, frozen and fearful.

No voice.

No well.

But I knew then that I would have to make my peace with the well, that I would have to see what lurked down there.

And I knew how I was going to find out.

"Mom."

"Oh, honey."

She started crying right away, sobbing.

"Honey, we've been so worried about you."

"I know, Mom. I'm sorry. I didn't kill Mae Swenson, Mom. I really didn't."

"We know that, son."

Then Dad came on the line. "The best thing you can do, Spence, is call the Chief and have him come and get you."

"I didn't do it, Dad."

"That isn't the point, honey."

He hadn't called me honey since I was eight or so. It felt right, though, in a corny endearing sort of way. I was his little boy again and he was scared as hell for me.

"Dad, is Josh there?"

"Sitting right here."

"I need to talk to him."

"Are you all right?"

"Pretty much. A little cold, I guess."

"You're not going to call the Chief are you?"

"Dad, if I call the Chief, he won't do any more investigating. He'll just assume I killed her. I've got an idea that might work. I at least need to try it."

"We're worried about you, Spence."

"I know, Dad. I love you and Mom very much but I really have to do this."

"It's your decision."

"Thanks, Dad."

He gave the phone to Josh.

"You think you could meet me at the line shack?"

"Sure."

I told him what to bring.

"All right," he said.

"You know what I can't figure out?"

"What?"

"Why Cindy hasn't talked to the Chief yet and told him that Garrett killed Mae Swenson."

There was a long silence. "Yeah, I guess it is kind of strange." He sounded a little funny when he said that but I thought it was the strain of the moment.

"You leaving now?" I said.

"Few minutes. But it'll take me a while to get there."

"How come?"

"Garrett follows me everywhere I go. I guess he thinks I'll lead him to you."

"That sonofabitch."

"So I'm going to take the old road, out past the saw mill, and get him good and lost, and then double back up to the line shack."

"Great."

"It'll take me a while, though."

"I know."

"I love you, Spence."

He'd never said that to me before; nor had I ever said that to him. Being on the run this way, so scared and confused all the time, had left me vulnerable. Soon as he said that, I had tears in my eyes.

"I love you, too, Josh."

"You want to talk to Mom and Dad again?"

"No, I'm standing in a spot where somebody could see me pretty easily. I'd better hang up."

"See you soon," he said.

"Thanks, Josh. Just be careful."

He laughed but I could tell he was nervous. "I'll even bring you the frozen Snickers I have in the fridge."

I laughed, too. "Just what I need tonight. Cold food."

5

It took him an hour and a half.

I waited up in a pine tree just behind the line shack. I could see everything in front of me for maybe a quarter mile. If anybody followed Josh, I'd be able to see them.

Josh came alone.

He had a paper bag tucked under his right arm and a huge flashlight waving from his left hand.

I swung down from the pine, the sweet scent of the juices filling my nostrils.

He didn't know where I was until he heard me land, and then he turned around as if he was going to jump me.

"It's me," I said, realising that he couldn't pick me out in the shadows beneath the tree.

"Scared the hell out of me."

"Sorry."

He came up to me and handed over the paper bag he was carrying. "Goodies," he said.

Heavier pair of gloves than the ones I was wearing, a couple of roast beef sandwiches, half a box of Oreos and a some dental floss.

I held up the little white plastic rectangle the floss was packaged in. "Now there's something every wanted fugitive needs – floss."

I guess I'd expected him to laugh. That's why I was so surprised when he looked hurt.

"Hey, Josh, I was just kidding."

"I did the best I could."

"Hey, listen, I really appreciate it."

"I just figured that after a day, you might like to floss. I hate it when I have stuff in my teeth."

"Aw, God," I said, and gave him a manly sock on the arm.

He was Josh the basketball star, and Josh the lady killer, but he was still, for a least moment every now and then, Josh my younger brother.

And it was sweet. Damned sweet.

"I really appreciate it," I said.

"Thanks. Mom and Dad didn't want me to bring you anything."

"Want me to just give up, huh?"

"Yeah. The man hunt is what scares them. Dad knows some of the men who're in it. They're kind of spooky guys."

"Yeah, they are."

"So I'm supposed to convince you to come back."

"I'd give up in a second if I was sure that Cindy had already talked to the Chief."

And there it was again.

The same nervous silence I'd heard when I'd brought up Cindy on the phone.

"There's something else in the sack," he said.

"Yeah, it felt a little heavy."

I opened the sack and stuck my hand way down and wrapped my hand around plastic-covered clothesline rope.

"That was the best I could do."

"It's great, Josh. It'll work fine."

"I'm just kind of surprised you're going to do it."

"I have to do it, Josh. Just to be sure."

"She's really got you going."

The way he said it, I realised for the first time that he didn't care much for Cindy.

He drifted over to the line shack, looked inside the empty doorway.

"Nice place you got here."

"Josh."

He pretended not to hear me. He knew what was coming.

He walked around the west side of the line shack and pounded on a few boards to see how sturdy they were.

"Josh."

Finally, he turned and said, "I don't want to talk about Cindy."

"Why not?"

"Because anything I say is just gonna hurt your feelings."

"Josh, I love her."

"I know that."

"And I think she loves me."

Silence.

"And I think she loves me."

"I think she loves herself," Josh said. "Not anybody else." He huddled deep into his pea jacket, a big, rangy Midwestern kid who managed to look knowing and naive at the same time.

"She'll go to the Chief and get me out of this mess. She said she would."

Another silence.

Then: "She isn't going to the Chief, Spence."

"How do you know that?"

"Because I asked her."

"You asked her?"

"I went over to see her right after dinner tonight."

"I didn't tell you to do that."

He looked irritated.

"No, you didn't tell me, Spence. But I decided to because I don't like the idea of my brother having to hide out in the woods."

He was hurt again.

"I'm sorry, Josh."

"After what you told me, about her and Garrett going out to Mae Swenson's and everything, I decided I'd go see her and ask her if I could take her to see the Chief."

"Yeah?"

"She said she didn't know what I was talking about. She said that she'd never had any conversation with you about Garrett, and that she'd thought about lying to help you out but she just couldn't bring herself to lie."

"God."

"Yeah," Josh said, "that's what I thought."

"She's my only hope."

He shook his head, came away from the shack, stood in the pale moonlight once again.

"No, you've got one other hope."

"What's that?"

"Garrett's apartment."

"I don't understand."

"He's at work now. Doesn't get through until after midnight. Then he usually spends an hour at Smiley's Tap playing bad-ass for all the barflies."

"We break in?"

He tapped his pea jacket. "I've got a glass cutter. I drove by his apartment a couple of times. He's got the whole downstairs. We should be able to get in the back door."

"Maybe we won't find anything."

"Maybe. But we've got to try."

"Yeah," I said. "Yeah, I guess we do."

"But we should get going."

I held up the coil of white plastic-sheathed clothesline rope. "In other words, you don't want me to check out the well?"

"I think it's pretty crazy."

"I have to know."

"All right. I just hope you don't slip and break your leg or something."

I smiled. "My brother, the optimist."

Once we got the rope securely tied to the crossbar under the hood of the well, I jumped up on the fieldstone that surrounded the well.

I had to duck down to move around but soon enough my gloved hands held the rope.

I slowly started to lower myself into the well.

Josh was there with his flashlight.

"It's pretty far down," he said. "The bottom, I mean."

"I'll be fine."

"Unless the monster gets you."

"Very funny."

I lowered myself a few more inches.

The interior of the well was the same dusty fieldstone below as up top. Various water levels had stained the stone over the years. Parts of the stone had worn smooth.

I didn't have to go far before I started getting feelings of claustrophobia. Premature burial. I read that Poe story when I was ten or so and was never able to forget it. Gave me nightmares for years. Closed in a coffin, slowly suffocating, screaming to get out, ripping my fingernails off as I clawed at the underside of the coffin lid –

I kept reminding myself that this was a very different reality.

My brother was up there with a flashlight. And any time I wanted to, I could start pulling myself up. And even if I got stuck somehow trying to get back up, Josh would lend a hand and make sure I made it.

My anger with Cindy also kept me from any morbid flights of premature fancy.

Why had she lied to Josh? Why wouldn't she help me when she knew very well I was innocent?

Why had she told me she was in love with me?

The smell started about halfway down. Think of sewer gas and that'll give you a pretty good idea. Sour, oppressive, filthy.

That was about when I heard it for the first time since I'd been in the well, that rumbling not-quite distinct voice, the voice of one of the ancient dark gods Lovecraft wrote about.

The further I descended, the louder the voice became.

I looked up.

Suddenly, Josh, the flashlight and safety seemed very far away.

I was nearing the bottom of the well now.

And the voice –

She was right, I thought. Cindy was right. About the well.

229

About the beast that could take over your will —

I could see the algae that was growing like a monstrous shining rug over the bottom of the well. I assumed that was part of the filthy smell.

I wondered what lay beneath all the fungus and other types of growth that made up the slimy green cloak —

Was that where the monster lurked?

The voice grew louder, louder and I felt my hands slip on the smooth plastic and —

I dropped at least four feet, afraid that I was going to drop straight into the growth below —

I stuck one of my feet out against the wall and stopped my fall. Then I wrapped the rope around my hands so I wouldn't fall again.

And then I stopped, stopped completely, and I just hung there and I heard the one thing I never ever *wanted* to hear but had feared all my life I *would* hear: silence.

Oh, I don't mean the silence of people not-talking; or the silence of being in a quiet room; or even the silence of deep night when you wake up suddenly and aren't quite sure where you are.

What I'm talking about is not merely the absence of noise — I'm talking about the *extinction* of all noise. Forever.

I've heard people on TV evangelism shows relate how one night they just had this religious experience, and, in less than a few seconds, came to know the true nature of the universe.

Personally, I never used to believe in that kind of thing, that sudden flash of wisdom, that cosmic hunch thing.

Well, what I was hearing was cosmic all right, but it was a lot more than a hunch. It was confirmation of the most terrifying thought of all...

I'd come to know the true nature of the universe, too, you see, at least that universe inhabited by all us woebegone folks of flesh and blood. We prefer fantasies of monsters and aliens and the drooling undead to the one absolute truth we don't want to face – that we are no better than possums or elephants or hissing, coiling snakes. We live and die without making any sense of our journey and then we face – extinction. Utter extinction. I mean, that's the nice thing about vampires and ghosts. They assure us that we can live on in some form or another. But if you want the truth, look at the poor raccoon dead on the side of the highway, or at the fine shiny casket hiding the corpse, or the skeletons that sometimes get washed from their graves in spring floods. There's the reality – extinction, and nothing else.

Cindy and David Myles and Garrett had convinced themselves that they heard voices telling them what to do because that implied that a higher power was controlling their lives. And a higher power, even a *dark* higher power, promised wonderful hushed secrets that assured them there would be no extinction, at least not for them, the chosen.

I wasn't sure whether to laugh or cry and maybe, in fact, I was doing a little bit of both as I hung down that smelly Midwestern well and saw how shabby and juvenile the fantasy had been, the fantasy about the well.

Voices, my ass.

Shared Psychotic Disorder.

Myles and Garrett had had the will to commit murder anyway. Cindy's game about the well simply gave them the courage to face their own desires.

I felt like a little boy who sat up in the dark all night staring at his closet, knowing that a monster waited for him on the other side of the door.

But when he opened it – nothing.

Absence. Extinction.

"You all right?" Josh shouted down.

"Yeah," I called up. "Unfortunately, I am."

"Huh?"

"I'll explain later."

I spent a few more moments listening. Oh, God, believe me,

I *wanted* to hear that rumbling voice again. I *wanted* to believe that dark and powerful forces could explain the heartbreaking vagaries of life on this forlorn planet of ours.

But I couldn't.

Because I'd learned the truth.

And the truth was a lot scarier than alien voices and caped creeping vampires.

I remembered the Hemingway story, 'A Clean, Well Lighted Place,' and the old man so afraid to die.

'Our *nada* who art in *nada*,' Hemingway says, '*nada* be thy name thy kingdom *nada* thy will be *nada* in *nada* as it is in *nada*.'

"You fucking lying sonofabitch," I said to the alien who did not dwell here, or dwell anywhere for that matter, "you fucking lying sonofabitch."

6

Garrett lived in the lower half of an old two-storey frame house. The place had once had some working class dignity but now the owners were young people who'd left two hot rods up on blocks to die right there on the front lawn. The house needed paint, the roof needed shingles, and several of the windows needed new panes.

We saw all this on our only drive past the front of the house. Then we parked two blocks away in an alley, pulled into an abandoned warehouse, and walked back to Garrett's place.

"You know how to use one of these puppies?" Josh said, showing me the glass cutter.

"I suppose we can figure it out," I said, turning it over in my hand.

"Long as he doesn't have some kind of security system, we should be all right."

We moved fast, not quite a run, and left black tracks in the white snow of the moon-bright alley.

When we got to the cross street, I hid behind a tree while Josh made sure that there was no traffic coming from either direction.

This time we did break into a run, and we kept it up until we stood, panting plumes of silver breath, on Garrett's back porch.

The porch smelled of garbage, due, no doubt, to the six large cans lined along the railing.

I tried the glass cutter first.

I had no trouble.

"Man, I can't believe that," Josh whispered, as I was opening the back door.

"Believe what?"

"The way you used that glass cutter."

"Why?"

"No offence, brother, but you're kind of a klutz."

Then there was no time for jokes.

We were inside.

The dominant smells were cigarette smoke, bourbon whiskey, old pizza cardboards, a bathroom that hadn't been cleaned in a while, and a few layers of Brut.

The furniture was all lumpy, old and done, like dead buffalos.

"You want the bathroom?" Josh said.

"Not if I don't have to."

He laughed. "You smelled it, too, huh?"

"I'm kidding. I'll take the bathroom and his room. You try the kitchen and the basement."

"Fine."

We were shadows, then, gliding through the street-lit darkness of these old-fashioned high-ceilinged rooms. Easy to imagine a player piano in the corner over there, and a family gathered round it singing 'Camptown Races' and 'Good Night, Irene.'

There was nothing much in the bathroom. I tried the closet, the medicine cabinet, the clothes hamper. Nothing useful I could find at all. Then I had to stop and wonder exactly what I was looking for. Garrett had already planted the knife in my car. The murder weapon rested in the Chief's office.

I was just leaving the bathroom when headlights suddenly stared in the front windows like the eyes of a wild animal.

I didn't move.

The headlights held there a long moment.

Josh came out of the kitchen, watched the lights, ready to run.

The sounds of a car radio; headlights dying. Car doors open and closing.

Footsteps coming toward the house.

"Damn," Josh said.

We both started to move to the back of the house when we heard the noise in the vestibule.

"Hey, cool it, man. The guy who lives downstairs is a cop."

"Big fuckin' deal."

"It'll be a big fuckin' deal if he decides to arrest ya."

"What can he arrest me for?"

"Cops can arrest ya for anything they want to arrest ya for."

"Bullshit."

"Bullshit, yourself."

"Shut up, you two. Let's get upstairs and eat this pizza."

"Remember, I ordered the half with the beef and hot peppers."

"You're really an asshole, you know that?"

This last line was spoken as they finally started climbing the stairs.

"God, how'd you like to hang out with those guys?" Josh grinned.

"Yeah, right."

"Let's start looking again."

I went into the bedroom and wished I hadn't.

First thing through the door, I smelled Cindy's perfume. I felt sick, thinking of them in the double bed that rested between two long corner windows.

I started hearing their ghosts, what she said to him, what he said to her.

She loves me, I wanted to say to Garrett's ghost.

But there wasn't time.

We had to hurry.

I started with his dresser drawers. One was filled with underwear, two handguns and several bullet clips. The next was filled with socks, a long economy-pack of Trojans, a small cellophane bag of stuff that looked and felt just like marijuana. The third drawer contained two ugly sweaters. Probably Christmas gifts he never wore. The last drawer held a bunch of skin magazines and several videotapes. *The Blonde Blower* was the title of one of the tapes. Kind of made a fella wonder what it was about.

I looked under the bureau and under the bed but found nothing. I looked behind the bed and behind the drapes and behind the small bookcase and found nothing again.

The closet seemed to hold no problem at all.

Garrett didn't exactly have a lot of clothes. There were three shirts on wire hangers that clanged, and maybe three pairs of dark slacks, and two pairs of Levi's. A fleece-lined jacket hung on one hook while a red and black checkered hunting shirt hung on another.

And then I saw them and I knew right away that something was wrong, him not wearing them tonight, and so I picked them up and I carried them out to the head of the basement.

"You down there?" I whispered.

"Yeah."

"I think I found something."

"What?"

"Bring the flashlight up."

That was the trouble with sharing a flashlight.

We put Garrett's new cowhide western boots down on the kitchen floor and then we started examining them.

There probably hadn't ever been a pair of western boots that had been examined with such care.

"Funny he isn't wearing these," I said. "They're his brand new boots."

"Yeah. Real funny."

"What if he didn't wear them because something was wrong with them?"

"That's what I was thinking."

"But what could be wrong with them?"

"I guess that's what we have to find out."

So we kept on looking.

Couple of times, the boys upstairs sounded as if they were standing on chandeliers and dropping big black vaults on the floor. And every so often they would swear at each other and argue about the pizza or the beer or the TV show they were watching. Fun guys.

Josh was the one to find it.

The white stitching on the upper part of the sole of the left boot.

The white stitching was discoloured maybe an inch, inch-and-a-half.

Josh held the beam close to the stitching.

"Kind've orange," he said.

"Yeah."

"The way dried blood is kind've orange sometimes."

"Maybe that's why he isn't wearing them."

Then we looked closer and saw that there was also a deep stain — like a splash — right across the arch of the same boot.

"Bet whatever stained the stitching also stained the arch," Josh said.

"I'd bet the same thing."

He turned off the flashlight.

We just knelt there in the faint moonlight, looking at the lone western boot sitting between us.

Josh said, "He gets Mae Swenson's blood on his boots —"

"— but he's too cheap to throw them away —"

"— so he just keeps them in the closet."

"Figuring that after I get convicted of her murder, he can start wearing his boots again."

"Maybe we're full of shit," he said.

"Maybe. But I don't think so."

"Neither do I."

"You know what I want to do with this boot?" he said.

"What?"

"Take it over to the Chief's office. Have somebody lock it up for the night. And you know what?"

"What?"

"I want you to come with me, brother."

"No way."

"It's time, brother. You can't keep running. Mom and Dad're

right."

We knelt there for a long time. Neither of us said anything.

Then he said, "I could beat the shit out of you."

"So?"

"So if I could beat the shit out of you, I can make you turn yourself in."

"Maybe you can't beat the shit out of me."

"Sure I can."

"It's crazy to turn myself in."

"No, it isn't, Spence. What's crazy is to keep running, and to let one of the local rednecks have an excuse for killing you."

I sighed. He was right.

"Scares the hell out of me," I said. "Turning myself in."

"Scares the hell out of me thinking about you out there all alone in the timber all night. Scares the hell out of Mom and Dad, too."

"How'd you ever get so grown up all of sudden."

"Vitamins."

I laughed. "You crazy asshole."

"Look who's talking."

7

In ten more minutes, the downtown stores would close. But for now, they looked lovely, all the electric Christmas lights and Santas and reindeer vivid against the night sky. Even the corny holiday music sounded good to me just then as we drove down the street toward the police station.

I was huddled deep down inside the collar of my coat, and hunched down in the seat. A lot of people were looking for me right now.

"How you doing?" he said.

"You mean other than pissing my pants?"

"Yeah, other than that."

"Other than that, just great."

"It's going to be all right, Spence. It really is. You just got to have a little faith."

"Uh-huh."

We were a block away from the police station when I saw her and when I saw her, I said, "Cindy!"

The library was right down the block from the police station. She'd probably been doing homework and was now walking home.

"Let me out so I can talk to her," I said.

"Are you crazy?" Josh said, grabbing at my arm because I'd already opened the door and was jumping out of the car even though it was still moving.

"We can walk from here!" I said. "Bring the boot!"

There wasn't anybody in the world I needed to see right now more than Cindy Marie Brasher. Nobody.

I was out the door and sliding ass-over-appetite on the icy street toward Cindy.

Behind me, I heard Josh cursing and pulling the car over to the kerb. It wasn't easy. I hadn't given him any warning.

She saw me then and she looked so sweet and beautiful in her navy blue tailored winter coat, her cheeks red with the season.

She looked confused, maybe even a little scared, as if she might want to drop her armload of textbooks and take off running.

But I reached the sidewalk before she could move.

"God," I said. "God, it's good to see you!"

She started to say something but I didn't let her. "I was so pissed off at you for not going to the Chief. But I'm not mad anymore, Cindy. I'm sure you were just scared."

I reached out and tried to take her in my arms but she very gently pushed me away.

"They're looking for you," she said.

"Right now, I don't give a damn, Cindy. All I give a damn about is talking to you."

"They say you killed Mae Swenson."

She had started to back away from me as we spoke.

"You know better than that, Cindy! You know I didn't kill her!"

Josh reached me just then and said, "C'mon, Spence, we've got to get going before somebody sees you."

I didn't pay any attention.

I tried to draw Cindy close to me again.

But once again she pushed away.

"We've got proof that Garrett killed her, Cindy. You don't even have to testify any more if you don't want to. Proof!"

I grabbed the western boot from Josh's hand and held it up to her. "There's blood on this boot. And once we get it analysed, I'm sure it'll be Mae Swenson's blood. And it's Garrett's boot!"

"Oh, shit," Josh said.

Only then did I become aware of a small group of people surrounding us. just gawking.

"It's Spence," a few of them whispered.

"They ain't gonna have a hard time findin' him now," one old-timer cackled.

But I didn't care.

This time, I pulled her to me so hard there was no way she could escape.

I felt as if I were stoned on the most exotic drugs I'd ever taken, drugs that somehow made Cindy my only reality.

I pulled her close enough to feel her soft sweet breath on my face.

"I'm going to take this boot to the Chief, Cindy, and then I'm going to be free. And then I'm going to wait for your graduation, and then we're going to get married. That's a promise, Cindy! That's a promise!"

I guess I saw the patrol car peripherally but it didn't really register until it came right tip over the kerb and stopped about three feet from where Cindy and Josh and I stood.

I turned and saw him get out of the car very quickly, his Magnum already drawn and ready for business. He had to move slowly because the sidewalk was very icy.

"No need in you getting hurt, Spence," Garrett said, looking crisp and efficient in his uniform. "I put the cuffs on you, put you in the back seat, that's all that's gonna happen."

"You sonofabitch," I said. "You're the one who should be arrested. You're the one who killed Mae Swenson, not me."

I could hear the growing crowd muttering about what I'd said.

But I didn't care what they thought either way.

Right now, all I wanted to do was get that boot safely to the Chief

Josh stepped up. "I was taking him to the police station, Garrett. You leave us alone, let us walk down that block alone, and you'll have him with no trouble."

Garrett smirked. "That right, little brother?"

"That's right. You have my word on it."

Garrett played to the crowd. "Now that's something isn't it? Your word on it? You think because you're some big basketball star, you can do whatever you want?"

A few crowd members laughed.

241

Garrett looked at Cindy. "He hurt you?"

She shook her head, mute.

"You ever lay a hand on her again, Spence, and I'll kill you right on the spot. You understand me?"

We'd come a long way from buying Conan comic books at the mall.

"May I go home?" Cindy said. "I'd really like to go home."

Garrett smiled at her and in that smile I could see that he loved her as much as I did. And for a moment, I almost felt sorry for him. Because Cindy was going to be mine.

The funny thing was, every few moments I'd be aware of that corny Christmas music on the air, and of the rusty noises the street decorations made when they blew in the wind.

"You go on home, Cindy. I'll call you later."

"Thanks," she said, and smiled nervously at him.

She looked at Josh and me as if we had crashed her party. This was the ultimate betrayal, taking Garrett's side here, but I couldn't help it. I still wanted to run away with her.

I had just turned back to Garrett when I saw his gaze light on the western boot that Josh carried in his right hand.

"What the hell's that?"

"None of your business," Josh said.

"None of my business. That's my boot you've got."

"We're taking it to the Chief," Josh said. "It's evidence."

"You two broke into my apartment tonight, didn't you?"

Josh nodded to me and said, "Just start walking to the station, Spence. I'll catch up with you."

"I want that boot," Garrett said.

Right now, I didn't exist for him. Neither did the swelling crowd, There was just him and Josh and that western boot.

"Go to the police station and turn yourself in, Spence," Josh said. "Don't give him an excuse to hurt you."

Garrett was moving closer all the time.

His Magnum was coming up and he was holding his free hand out, palm up.

"Put the boot right there, hero. And right now."

"You're not getting it," Josh said. Then to me, "Get going, Spence. Turn yourself in."

"I'm not going to tell you again, asshole. The boot. Now."

And that was when he lunged for it, Garrett did.

And that was when he lost it, totally lost it. It must have been the boot that made him so crazy, how the boot would ultimately give him away.

And that was when it happened, the gun going off, the gun I still hear and will hear for the rest of my life, the gun that put three bullets into the chest of my brother Josh, and left him dead upon the sidewalk.

I don't remember most of it, just holding Josh and rocking him and rocking him, and crying his name over and over and over.

I guess I was aware of Garrett getting into his patrol car and driving away but it didn't matter to me.

Not with my little brother Josh dead in my arms. Not with Josh dead in my arms.

Seven Years Later

1

On the day they execute him, my wife Cindy wakes before me and goes into the bathroom and throws up. The noise and grief of it wakes me. I roll over, eyes just opening, and see the grey harsh sky filling the window.

Down the hall, the oldest of our two children, Marisa, age four, is calling out for her mother. She is sobbing.

I tug on my pyjama bottoms and trot down the hall. Marisa is subject to very bad nightmares and needs constant reassurance that everything in her world is going to be all right.

Susan is still sleeping in her crib as I sit down on the edge of Marisa's bed and put her in my lap. She is sleep-warm, sleep-sweet. I feel ashamed to admit this, even to myself, but she is my favourite daughter. I cannot help the way I feel.

Her pyjama top is wet from her tears. She hugs me.

"I heard him, Daddy, I heard him," she sobs into my neck.

"Heard who, honey?"

"The man in the well."

My entire body freezes.

"Did your Mommy take you there again?"

"Uh-huh."

"When?"

"Yesterday. And he was in my dreams, Daddy. The man in the well. And he talked to me."

"I'm sorry, honey. But you're all right. He can't hurt you."

She is sniffling now, the worst of her tears over with. "He scares me, Daddy."

"I know, honey. I know he does." Then I hoist her up and bounce her in the air the way I did when she was Susan's age. "How about some Frosted Flakes?"

I make her breakfast: her favourite cereal, Frosted Flakes, a small glass of orange juice, a Flintstones vitamin, and a piece of wheat toast with jam (she hates both margarine and butter).

"Now you sit here and enjoy your breakfast. I'm going to go talk to your mommy."

She is naked in the bathroom, just stepping out of the shower when I open the door and let myself in without knocking.

"That's not very nice," she says. If anything, the seven years have made her more beautiful, given her face a richer, more melancholy beauty.

"Neither is taking Marisa to the well."

She looks away quickly, reaches out for her blue robe hanging on the back of the door. She can't quite reach it. I watch the way her breasts ride up as her arm stretches. Unfortunately, she seems to have lost her sexual desire of late. We make love a few times a month and she's developed the habit of taking a shower immediately after the deed is done, as if she wants all memory of me washed away.

I hold the robe for her and she turns her back to me and slides into the buff blue terrycloth.

I watch our faces in the mirror.

"You promised," I said.

"Little children love fantasy games."

"Not this fantasy game. She's terrified of it."

She stares at my reflection a long time and says, "Well, life's sort of a terrifying business, anyway, isn't it?"

This last time, the fourth since our wedding, she stayed in the hospital six weeks. At least this time there was no electroshock. I'm not sure she ever quite recovered from them.

"Don't you have to be at your parents'?" Cindy says.

"Yes."

An ironic smile in the mirror. "I'd tell you to give them my best but I guess they probably wouldn't want to hear that, would they?"

"No."

Then she pauses and turns around and takes me in her arms. As we're kissing, I smell her clean wet hair and her damp sumptuous flesh and the faint hint of her sex. How I love to worship in that particular grotto.

She hasn't kissed me like this in months and I'm flustered. Can't help it. Have an erection that is driving me absolutely crazy.

"I really want to get fucked tonight," she says, in a voice I've never quite heard before.

"That makes two of us."

She pulls me to her once again and slips her hand easily inside my pyjama bottoms.

She takes my cock out and begins to slip it up between her legs. She is wet down there, too, but it is a more profound and silken wetness than mere water.

Half an hour later, I am sitting in my parents' living room. They are both on the couch, sitting very straight and very close together.

We are all well aware of what day this is.

They are old well beyond their years, my parents. It is not the age of time but the age of sorrow. They will never recover from the murder of my brother. They are both heavily tranquillised most of the time. If they ever desert their medicine, they are given to long periods of frightening depression.

"That god damned governor better not pardon him," my father says.

"He won't," my mother says. "Don't you worry."

"How are the kids?" my father says.

"Good."

"She ever going to let you bring them over?"

That is how they refer to her. 'She.' Never by name. They blame her for my brother's death.

Their reasoning goes thusly: if I hadn't gone out with Cindy, I would not have been accused of murder, and if I had not been accused of murder, Josh would not have been on the street corner where Garrett, the real murderer, killed him. Not even when I point out that she testified against Garrett – was an eyewitness to not only Josh's murder but to Mae Swenson's – not even then do they care. They just say that she was protecting herself, that's the only reason she co-operated with the County Attorney.

They absolutely refuse to see her.

They would not attend our wedding, the baptism of the girls, or any holidays if 'she' was to be present.

I think back to the day, seven years ago, when I told my father that I had been seeing her without them knowing it, and that I had asked her to marry me. He said, "Never bring that cunt in my house." I had never heard him use that word before. It had a shocking effect on me.

Now, on this day, my mother says, "They should have two gurneys, side by side."

"One for him," my father says, "one for her."

"If she goes into the mental hospital again," my mother says, "you should try to get permanent custody of those kids. We'd be happy to have them stay here."

"As long as she never tries to come over here," he says.

I get up. I can't do this any longer.

My father says, "You don't care that she helped murder your little brother, do you?"

"She didn't help murder him, Dad," I say wearily.

"Far as I'm concerned," my mother says, "she should be right next to him on another gurney."

"She's a fucking whore," my father says. He's just starting to shout now. The shouting will last for as long as I stay. Once he starts to shout at me, he can't stop.

"She's a fucking whore, you know that, Spence? Your wife's a fucking whore!"

2

I am at the Earl May Gardening centre, picking up some peat moss. Spring has touched the world again.

I am loading the bags in the trunk of my station wagon when I sense somebody standing next to me.

I look up and see my father.

I have not seen him for three months. In that time he seems to have aged a decade. His eyes look like blind eyes and both his hands twitch as if with palsy.

But the smirk is the most disturbing part.

He pokes at me with a sharp gnarled finger. "You hear what your little whore did last week?"

He is not going to let me speak.

"She went up to the old line shack with the Sievers boy, that big strapping football star who plays at State?"

The smirk becomes almost insane with pleasure.

"She fucked him. Right against the well. She probably fucked you that way, too, right, standing up against the well?"

"God, Dad, you got bad information. She isn't like that. She really isn't."

"Uh-huh," he says. "Uh-huh. Well, Doe Parson happened to see 'em with his very own eyes. He was out there with his birds the way he usually is and he saw them plain as day. That little whore of yours and the football boy!"

And then he breaks and begins sobbing and everybody in the sunny parking lot starts looking at us and all I can do is throw my arms around this ancient and aggrieved figure – but he pushes me away, pushes through a few onlookers, and wobbles away to the front of the store.

3

Six evenings later, Cindy having taken Marisa to the mall, I decide to do it, do what I've been thinking about ever since I saw my father in the parking lot.

I search through her bureau.

And there I find it – tucked under a stack of family photographs – a very glossy snapshot of the Sievers boy in his State uniform, holding up a football as if he's about to make a touchdown pass.

On the back, he's written a note.

"To my all-time favourite teacher."

I do not have to wonder what it is she has taught him.

I do not have to wonder at all.

CT Publishing

If you have enjoyed this book, we are quietly
confident you will enjoy the following titles as well.

ED GORMAN
NIGHT KILLS

The odd thing was how comfortably she seemed to fit inside there, as if this were a coffin and not a freezer at all. She was completely nude and only now beginning to show signs of the freezing process, ice forming on her arms and face.

But he could tell she hadn't been in here very long because of the smells...

Frank Brolan, successful adman, unwitting fall-guy. Someone has murdered a call girl and planted her in his freezer. Frank has to find the killer before the cops find him.

As the body count rises, with the killer leaving Frank's mark at every crime, Frank flees into the night and the city. He finds help in an unlikely duo—a teenage whore and a wheelchair-bound dwarf with a mind like a steel trap...

"A painfully powerful and personal novel about three outsiders—an alcoholic advertising executive, a man twisted and disfigured by spina bifida, and a runaway teenage girl—brought together in a noir unlike any you've ever read. Violent, melancholy, bitterly humorous, Night Kills is a 'relationship' novel of the classic mould. As disturbing and sad a crime novel as I've ever read."

–CEMETERY DANCE

Price: £4.99 ISBN: 1-902002-03-2
Available from all good bookshops, or post free from: CT Publishing, PO Box 5880, Birmingham B16 8JF
Email ct@crimetime.demon.co.uk

GWENDOLINE BUTLER
COFFIN IN OXFORD

"It was like a Chinese puzzle. In St Ebbe's was a flat, in the flat was a trunk, and in the trunk was a body. The body of a woman..."

Ted was brought round from the first attack, if you could call it an attack, with difficulty. He had been found shut up in a cupboard with a scarf tightened around his neck: his own scarf, to add insult to injury...

'Gwendoline Butler is excellent on the bizarre fantasies of other people's lives and on modern paranoia overlaying old secrets; and her plots have the rare ability to shock'
ANDREW TAYLOR, THE INDEPENDENT

ISBN: 1-902002-00-8 Price: £4.99

JENNIE MELVILLE
WINDSOR RED

Charmian Daniels, on a sabbatical from the police force takes rooms in Wellington Yard, Windsor near the pottery of Anny, a childhood friend. The rhythm of life in Wellington Yard is disturbed by the disappearance of Anny's daughter with her violent boyfriend. Dismembered limbs from an unidentified body are discovered in a rubbish sack. A child is snatched from its pram. Headless torsos are found outside Windsor.

Are these events connected? And what relationship do they have to the coterie of female criminals that Charmian is 'studying'...? All is resolved in a Grand Guignol climax that will leave the most hardened crime fiction fans gasping.

ISBN: 1-902002-01-6 Price: £4.99

Available from all good bookshops, or post free from:
CT Publishing, PO Box 5880, Birmingham B16 8JF